PRAISE FOR S*.*

"Sid Balman's story c([...]
acters and descripti([...]
I could almost feel [...]
West Point uniform. [...]
struggle with radicali [...]
understanding of the [...]
claims them, and the necessity to tackle this challenge with
more finesse than we currently muster."
— **Kimberly C. Field**, Brigadier General USA (ret) and
Former Deputy Assistant Secretary of State for
Conflict and Stabilization

"An authentic and powerful take on the living, beating heart of
multiculturalism in America and a nuanced journey through
the lives of families whose destinies are intertwined over
multiple generations. If you are a fan of prestige television
like Dynasty, but also enjoy strong political thrillers like I
do, then this is the book for you! Refreshingly original and
important, from the compelling cover art to the final word."
— **Mustafa Hasnain**, founder Creative Frontiers;
Lahore, Pakistan

"*Seventh Flag*'s rapid paced narrative takes readers from
the football fields of West Texas to the battlefields of the
Middle East; from Mexican shootouts to an Ashram in India.
A former war correspondent, Balman's lively prose has his
audience inside a tank's turret and with the media cluster in
the rear of the Secretary of State's aircraft. The book enter-
tains and enlightens!"
— **US Ambassador James Bishop** (Ret.)

"A must read! *Seventh Flag* views the world through the eyes of two very different families as they move through the trials and tribulations that we are currently experiencing across different societies and religions. Their journey together helps them appreciate the different challenges and choices individuals must make, the importance of family and their common humanity."
—**Shaykh Siddiqi**, Founder Hijaz College; and The Blessed Guide of the Naqshbandi Hijazi Sufi Order

"Think you know what shapes Texas? Sid Balman's tale of a *Seventh Flag* over Texas will rattle what you think. This saga of a generational partnership "as unlikely as the idea of a United States" is rooted in a true event from before the Civil War that led to Texas, of all places, being home to more Muslim Americans than any other state."
—**Mark Stein**, *New York Times* bestselling author of *How the States Got Their Shapes*

SEVENTH FLAG

SEVENTH
FLAG

A NOVEL

SID BALMAN JR.

SPARKPRESS

Published by SparkPress, a BookSparks imprint,
A division of SparkPoint Studio, LLC
Phoenix, Arizona, USA, 85007
www.gosparkpress.com

Published 2019
Printed in the United States of America
ISBN: 978-1-68463-014-1 (pbk)
ISBN: 978-1-68463-015-8 (e-bk)

Library of Congress Control Number: 2019939205

Cover illustration by Yahya Ehsan, Creative Frontiers 2019
Interior design by Tabitha Lahr

There are no words to adequately thank my family for their support: Elena, Sidney, Mia, Estrella, Rue, and Barbara, the strongest woman of them all.

EPIGRAPH

Quis ut Deus?
Who is like God?
Revelation 12:7

When earth is rocked in her last convulsions; when earth shakes off her last burdens and man asks, "What may this mean?" On that day she will proclaim her tidings, for your Lord will have inspired her.

On that day mankind will come in broken hands to be shown their labors. Whoever has done an atom's weight of good shall see it, and whoever has done an atom's weight of evil shall see it also.

—The Qur'an

DISCLAIMER

Seventh Flag is a work of historical fiction. Some of the characters, organizations, events, places, timing, and stories are authentic, although minor liberties may have been taken regarding dates, names, and dialogue. The major characters and their lives are entirely fictitious, patched together through the true experiences of many individuals and my imagination. While great care has been exerted to respect and to observe the traditions of Islam, including detailed consultations with Muslim scholars, it is a complex faith with many interpretations, and I apologize in advance for any unintentional miscues.

FAMILY TREE

Laws Family

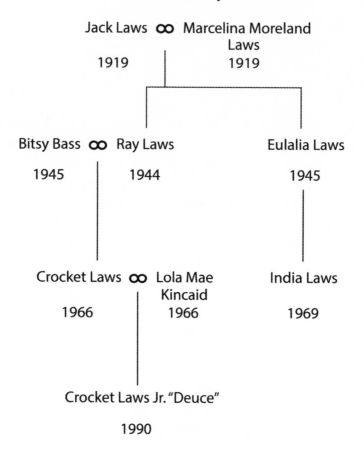

Jack Laws ∞ Marcelina Moreland Laws
1919   1919

Bitsy Bass ∞ Ray Laws   Eulalia Laws
1945   1944   1945

Crocket Laws ∞ Lola Mae Kincaid   India Laws
1966   1966   1969

Crocket Laws Jr. "Deuce"
1990

Zarkan Family

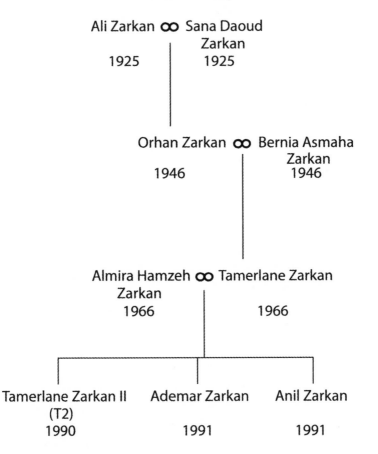

Ali Zarkan ∞ Sana Daoud
Zarkan
1925   1925

Orhan Zarkan ∞ Bernia Asmaha
Zarkan
1946   1946

Almira Hamzeh ∞ Tamerlane Zarkan
Zarkan
1966   1966

Tamerlane Zarkan II   Ademar Zarkan   Anil Zarkan
(T2)
1990   1991   1991

PROLOGUE

A ndrew Solomons has come a long way from the tweedy academics at Brown University in the 1940s to the high desert of West Texas almost twenty years after the turn of the next century. He has no regrets, and he didn't mind the occasional pilgrimage ninety miles west on US 62 across what was once Comanche country to attend synagogue in El Paso during those years when he felt the need to atone for something.

Solomons stares through the glass walls of his office into the small newsroom of the *Hudspeth County Herald* in Dell City, a far cry from the cavernous hubbub of the *New York Times*, where—as a young man in Providence making a pain in the ass of himself sniffing out scoops for the *Brown Daily Herald*—he imagined a career. *No tweed here*, he thinks, rather a Scully vest, jeans, a ranger belt, and a pair of Justin work boots. The only homage to journalism is an old Underwood typewriter—one of those *clickety-clack* black throwbacks over which editors in sleeve garters once chain-smoked and banged out copy—he bought at the dollar store and perched on a shelf in the corner as a reminder of sorts of his principles, and of his dreams.

Solomons feels a nap creeping up on him, like old men do in the late afternoon on a cold day when they forget to eat lunch or, in his case, didn't make it to Rosita's before closing time at two. He longs for one of those smoked brisket sand-wiches, or a plate of huevos rancheros that will burn through him during the next morning's ablutions. But he fights sleep and hunger to reflect on the stories and people that have pop-ulated his life. Age has taken plenty, but not that, not yet.

His world has been dominated by the evolution of this particular corner of West Texas. Sure, there were the mun-dane accounts of the highs and lows of the Dell City Cougars' six-man football team, acrobatic air shows, the occasional farm accident, a marriage or birth, trophy bucks, and 4-H compe-titions. But there were some big stories too: a Texas Supreme Court ruling on water rights worth hundreds of millions of dollars, campaign visits on whistle-stop tours by presiden-tial candidates, desperadoes of all varieties crisscrossing the Chihuahuan Desert with all imaginable kinds of contraband, heroes who had served and died in every conflict since World War II, and even a brush with Middle Eastern terrorists. Life in Dell City followed the arc of a nation whose people served as a beacon of optimism and opportunity after World War II but, over the next eight decades, lost that innocence in a world where radicalism metastasized into every community.

In Solomons's mind, two families framed it all: the Laws, quintessential Americans who helped found Dell City and operated one of the largest farms for decades; and the Zarkans, descendants of Syrian Muslims who brought camels across the ocean in the 1800s for the US Army and worked with the Laws for generations. Their partnership was as unlikely as the idea of a United States, and their powerful friendship can be traced back to a bloody knife fight in a Juarez cantina just after World War II. Jack Laws, the hard-edged patriarch of the family, hired Solomons after the war to launch the *Hudspeth County Herald* because his wife, Marcelina, a trailblazer in her own right and one of those Texas women who has a way with a petticoat as well as a 30.30, had a sense that the history of Dell City and its people would be important. *As always,* he thinks, *Marcelina was right.*

Texas, Solomons thinks, *there's been six flags that have flown over you: Spain, France, Mexico, the Republic of Texas, the Confederate States of America, and the United States.* But, in Texas today, he imagines a seventh flag—not one of a state or a nation but one that represents a mosaic of cultures, religions, and people from every corner of the world struggling to define what it means to be unified as Americans under an ambiguous banner.

PART
ONE

CHAPTER 1

Senator Jefferson Davis of Mississippi had a pet project. But even as the respected chairman of the Committee on Military Affairs, he found it difficult to win the support of fellow lawmakers. Davis's hopes for the idea had been renewed since President Franklin Pierce appointed him secretary of war after his inauguration in 1853. Pierce was known as an innovator, due in part to being the youngest president in history at forty-seven. Davis could certainly see plenty of evidence to support that notion as he buttoned his trousers in the newly renovated bathroom on the second floor of the White House and washed his hands with warm water, made possible by the addition of a hot water furnace that was almost unheard of in most buildings at the time.

Davis greeted the president warmly as he walked into his private office next to the Cabinet Room on the second floor.

"Good morning, Mr. President."

"Jeff," Pierce acknowledged, motioning him to sit down at the oak coffee table, in the middle of which sat two china coffee cups and the secretary of war's recent report to Congress, opened to a page where a passage had been underlined.

[In the] Department of the Pacific, the means of transportation have, in some instances, been improved, and it is hoped further

developments and improvements will still diminish this large item of our army expenditure. In this connection . . . I again invite attention to the advantages to be anticipated from the use of camels and dromedaries for military and other purposes, and for reasons set forth in my last annual report, recommend that an appropriation be made to introduce a small number of the several varieties of this animal, to test their adaptation to our country. . . .

"Ships of the desert," said the president, using a common nickname for camels.

"They drink up to twenty gallons of water at a time, and that hump is twenty pounds of fat that can keep them going for a week in the desert. Find me an army mule that can do that. Camels are ideal for our troops out there in Texas and the New Mexico Territories."

President Pierce held up his hand, cutting Davis short. "I like it, and for thirty thousand dollars how can we go wrong?"

A year later Congress enacted the Shield Amendment and appropriated ". . . *the sum of $30,000 . . . under the direction of the War Department in the purchase and importation of camels and dromedaries to be employed for military purposes.*"

Within months, the navy store ship USS *Supply*, under the command of Lt. David Dixon Porter, loaded the first shipment of camels—nineteen cows and fourteen bulls for which they paid $250 each—from exotic ports in Tunis, Egypt, Turkey, and Malta, along with several dozen handlers to tend them. Among them was a twenty-four-year-old Syrian named Hadji Ali, whom the soldiers nicknamed Hi Jolly for his sunny disposition and occasional pranks, and his sidekick, Mustafa Zarkan. They had a way of cheering the crew up during the storm-tossed, three-month voyage to Indianola, Texas, on the Gulf of Mexico 140 miles south of Houston.

Mustafa Zarkan was a burly man with an unusually thick neck for a desert Arab, and he never seemed to tire. He had been a champion wrestler in the Syrian town of Palmyra, something he had kept secret until just the right moment during the voyage. One calm evening about three weeks into the journey, he nailed a sign to a mast announcing a wrestling challenge to "all comers." Zarkan spoke English fairly well, but he had to let Lt. Porter in on the scheme in order to come up with the right words for the sign. Aloysius Hart, a barrel-chested corporal who had become a friend to both Syrian crewmembers and shown interest in their Muslim faith, was the first to step into the wrestling circle. Within seconds, Zarkan had spun Al around, thrown a headlock on him, and pinned him to the deck. Man after man tried their luck with him, all with pretty much the same outcome. "Zarkan wrestling" became a favorite on the ship, and Mustafa would regularly hold training sessions in which he would instruct the men on the intricacies of grappling.

Just a few months after their arrival, the army's experiment began to show promise, with the camels able to tote almost four hundred pounds at four miles an hour without needing anywhere near as much water as horses or pack mules. And the cost of upkeep was far less for camels, which could live on Texas mountain cedar and creosote bush that was indigestible by the other pack animals. Within four years, the US Army and some independent businessmen had imported several thousand more dromedaries to the American West. But they were surly and didn't get along with horses, characteristics that advocates argued would keep Indians at bay, but which didn't sit well with the troops.

The US Camel Corps ultimately failed in part as a result of that ornery disposition and of the cavalry's affection for horses but mostly due to the onset of the Civil War. In 1867, Secretary of War Edwin M. Stanton ended the costly experiment, concluding that "I cannot ascertain that these have ever been so employed as to be of any advantage to the Military Service." The remaining camels were auctioned at about $31 each, mostly to circuses, miners, and prospectors.

Hi Jolly and Mustafa Zarkan eventually arranged marriages with families in Syria, like many of the Arabs involved with the US Camel Corps. And a fair number settled in and around El Paso, which grew to become one of the largest concentrations of Muslims in Texas. Hi Jolly put down roots in Quartzite, Arizona, and Governor Benjamin Moeur dedicated a monument there to him and to the US Camel Corps. In 1935, Moeur unveiled an almost fifteen-foot, pyramid-shaped stack of granite stones with a steel camel silhouetted on top and a plaque inscribed: "The last camp of Hi Jolly, born somewhere in Syria about 1828; died at Quartzite December 16, 1902. Came to this country February 10, 1856. Camel driver—Packer—Scout—over thirty years a faithful aide to the US Government."

CHAPTER 2

In 1948, Dell City was ground zero for the agricultural gold rush, and veterans of World War II blew across the desert like the sand that pelted their canvas tents to find steady work and to chase the American dream in the wide-open West. It was a melting pot of cultures, stirred by hundreds of Latin braceros living outside town at Camp 16, who had journeyed across the border legally under the US–Mexico Farm Labor Agreement for plentiful work and more money than they could make in a decade busting sod in the poor rural villages of Chihuahua, Coahuila, Nuevo Leon, or Tamaulipas.

Jack Laws, the grandson of an Irish immigrant who had fled the dank basements and cholera outbreaks of Boston for the Central Valley of California, was different from most of them, with a vision and money to get it started. Jack had arranged financing in 1944 for the purchase of sixty thousand acres at about two million dollars and was proud to be thought of as a founding father of Dell City. Jack's employees appreciated the work he provided and the way he kept their families happy with a diversion on Sunday besides church. On this Sunday, he had brought some of his old military buddies together to perform an air show, and most of the town had gathered on makeshift bleachers to watch.

Sheriff E. A. "Doggie" Wright and Texas Ranger Bob Coffey stood in front of the crowd delivering a preview for the show, which included seventeen aircraft from three counties: Hudspeth, El Paso, and Culbertson. Most of the planes, high-wing Luscombe 8s and Piper J3 Cubs, were used as crop dusters or to carry predator bounty hunters after coyotes that were ravaging livestock on ranches in the Chihuahuan Desert. Today, Coffey explained, they would be "putting on a display of high-altitude acrobatics."

"Death defying," Sheriff Wright proclaimed.

As a pilot pulled the blocks from behind the Piper, a man stumbled out of the crowd with a half-empty bottle of Jack in one hand and began making a nuisance of himself, not entirely unheard of on a Sunday afternoon in Dell City. Weaving around a bunch of airplanes was no place for an inebriated cowboy, and a deputy tried to shepherd him away from what could be a calamity, or worse. But the drunk broke free and made for the Piper. As he grabbed the keys from the pilot, jumped into the cockpit, and fired up the engine, the crowd gasped and scattered for whatever cover they could find in the cholla cactus and mesquite. Only Jack, the sheriff, and the ranger were in on the joke, and they stayed put.

It became clear with his first chandelle over the crowd that a big gag had been played on everyone, and the people settled back into their seats for a few hours of *oohing* and *aahing* at the flying circus. Andrew Solomons had been there too and had written a lighthearted story in the *Herald*, illustrated with a photograph of the whiskey bottle on the ground a few feet behind the Piper as it started rolling down the dirt runway, headlined "'High' Flier in Dell City."

Jack had a wicked Irish sense of humor, you bet, as well as a pair of sparkling blue eyes and big ears that made him look a bit like an overgrown leprechaun. But he had a temper, too, and was not above wading into a fistfight if he got his dander up. It was those blue eyes that won the heart of Marcelina Moreland when they first met in the California Central Valley, where Jack had some farmland and Marcie, who had graduated with an agriculture degree from Texas A&M in the 1930s, worked as a water specialist for Archer Daniels Midland, one of the first women to rise in the ranks at ADM.

Marcie, who had grown up in West Texas, understood men well enough to navigate a career during a time when the phrase "glass ceiling" hadn't been invented yet. She was nobody's patsy, choosing her battles carefully and not making a federal case every time she was asked to fetch coffee. And she knew water, a respected expert who consulted on ADM's most important projects. That's why they sent her to the Central Valley during the final stages of the "water wars" over rights to the Owens River. To the detriment of smallholder farmers like Jack, the Owens River had been diverted to quench thirsty Los Angelinos and nourish palm trees along Mulholland Drive, named after William Mulholland, who engineered the entire scheme. Jack didn't have much luck raising potatoes, but before enlisting in the navy and marrying Marcie, she convinced him to switch to cotton, and he was making a pretty good run at it.

A 7.7 mm round from the nose gun of a Japanese A6M Zero took Jack's right thumb clean off as they were transporting American soldiers to the beaches of New Guinea. He returned to California and to Marcie, determined to find a place to farm where he could be the master of his own destiny, and maybe even find a little oil. They pored over maps, reviewed land titles, and studied the agronomies from California to Texas, finally narrowing down their list to Hudspeth County, not far from where Marcie had grown up, and Henderson, Nevada. In retrospect, Henderson, sixteen miles south of Las Vegas, would have made Jack millions on the real estate play alone. And water could be an issue in West Texas, although Marcie was convinced that snowmelt running off the nearby Sacramento Mountains into the hundred-square-mile Bone Springs–Victorio Peak Aquifer under Dell City would give them all they needed.

Marcie, eager to raise a family near home, favored Texas, and she had a way of winning Jack over to her side. Marcie had a tiny wild streak that she kept under wraps, and she could be flirtatious when the mood struck her. As teenagers, she and her friends had consumed books and magazines considered racy for the times and paid close attention to any tips that might fill in gaps of the sterile talks their mothers gave them on the birds and the bees. She had read something in a D. H. Lawrence novel about how some men enjoy a dominant woman, and late one night in bed, she surprised Jack by climbing on top, guiding him inside her, and pinning his arms.

"You like this ride, cowboy?" Marcie asked playfully as she rocked slowly back and forth.

"Huh."

"You like?"

"Yes."

"I think you'd like it a lot better in Texas."

"You win," he moaned, and they melted into each other, the matter of where they would live settled.

Nine months later, Ray was born, and Eulalia followed within two years. Nursing Eulalia on the porch swing overlooking the sprawling farm in Dell City, nobody was happier than Marcie, except maybe Jack on those cold January nights under a Pendleton blanket with his wife.

CHAPTER 3

A lmost a century after Mustafa Zarkan set foot on the Texas shore with a shipment of unruly camels, his great-grandson, Ali Zarkan, was picking cotton in the fields of West Texas, a broken man and a fallen Muslim.

He was often mistaken in Camp 16 outside Dell City for one of the braceros, Latino migrants who worked legally under the US–Mexico Farm Labor Agreement. He never corrected that impression, since his Spanish was good enough to pass for a Mexican, and he certainly didn't want anyone knowing the truth. Ali had fought and killed Japanese soldiers in the stinking jungles of the Western Pacific, staring many of them straight in the eye as he rammed a trench knife into their gut or slashed it across their jugular. He had lost his way during those army years—with all the killing and the booze—and his faith. After the war, Ali had returned to his family in Arizona, but he couldn't stick with it, couldn't stand the pitying way they looked at him when he smoked on the porch while they knelt for Salah, the compulsory prayers Muslims perform five times daily facing east toward the holy city of Mecca. Ali drifted across the desert southwest, like a dried-out tumbleweed, making enough money to keep drifting by pumping gas or winning a few dollars bludgeoning drunken cowboys in bare-knuckle fights behind dive bars from Las Cruces to Alpine. He was a *kafir*, one who hides the truth, unclean and undeserving. *Or maybe* drunk *was a better word*, Ali thought, given the way he threw back tequila and whored across the bridge from El Paso in the seedy neighborhoods of Juarez. Ali felt he deserved this life of shit, living in a ramshackle dormitory outside Dell City with a dozen or so men, unwashed most of the time and working dawn to dusk picking vegetables or bailing cotton for Jack Laws.

Jack was good to his workers, as good as a non-union outfit could be to a bunch of mostly itinerant American and Mexican laborers in West Texas during the late 1940s, and he seemed to take a special liking to Ali, or Alberto, as Ali called himself to hide his roots. The first time they shook hands, Ali noticed Jack's missing thumb, and Jack recognized the look in Ali's eyes that he'd seen in so many of the soldiers they picked off the beaches of the Western Pacific after months of combat, of gore.

"Lost it to a Jap fighter."

"New Guinea?"

"Yeah."

"I saw my share over there."

"It shows."

So much was said with a few words, in the way that men—particularly quiet men—communicate, and from that point forward, Jack seemed to gravitate toward Ali.

Jack would have appreciated Ali's company well after midnight on a Friday at El Recreo, a dive bar in Juarez a few blocks from the center of town, off Calle Ignacio Mejia. Jack was alone, just spending time with himself, nursing a Bohemia after a few shots of mezcal—feeling no pain—when three drunken "rhinestone" vaqueros came blowing into the bar like they owned the place. *Trouble*, Jack thought, and pulled his Marfa Low Crown lower over his green eyes as the bartender discreetly moved as many glasses off the bar as he could. One of the vaqueros, the one in the polished black cowboy boots with silver-tipped, needle-nose toes, jostled Jack as they sidled up to the bar on either side of him and ordered a bottle of tequila "*lo mejor.*"

"*Con permiso, cabron,*" he said, emphasis on *cabron*, dumbass.

As usual, Jack couldn't contain the angry Irishman in him. "Fuck you."

Time seemed to slow down for Jack at that exact moment, as it had when the Japanese zero had come in low over the Pacific Ocean just offshore from New Guinea, nose gun firing 7.7 mm chunks of steel, and taken his thumb. Jack barely had time to duck before he caught a glancing blow from one of the vaqueros, but it was square enough to knock him off the chair with a flash in his head, and stars. He heard the click of a switchblade and saw another vaquero moving to him fast but methodically, weaving the blade from side to side as men do who know how to fight with knives and who have killed with them. His thoughts were of Marcie, the kids, and how his big Irish mouth had landed him in the shit again. But something else caught his eye, moving quick and low and quiet from a shadow in the corner of the room. The vaquero with the blade flew over the bar, and his weapon clattered to the wooden floor. The head of another vaquero, the fat one who had been laughing, jerked to the side at an unnatural angle, and jagged chunks of what had been three gold teeth clattered on the floor just before his head bounced off the Mexican tile with a sharp crack. The switchblade suddenly reappeared in the hand of the stranger who had stepped between Jack and the last vaquero, and he moved forward, grasping the knife in a clenched fist, blade down, as military combat instructors teach in basic training.

"*Amigo, patron, por favor!*"

The stranger said something that sounded to Jack like "abracadabra" and then sunk the full blade of the knife deep into the chest of the vaquero, who dropped like a Raggedy Andy—probably not dead since the blade was too short to pierce his heart or lungs. Jack clambered to his feet, not knowing who the stranger was but damn sure to get him out of there and across the border for a proper thank you before the police threw them into El Cereso Prison, where the only law was the law of the jungle, and they'd have to fight or end up as bitches for some gang.

The stranger turned toward Jack, and he immediately recognized Ali.

"Jesus!"

"No, Alberto."

Jack tossed a twenty-dollar bill on the bar as the two men stepped over the bodies and disappeared into the Juarez night. Not a word was said until they crossed the Zaragoza Bridge over the Rio Grande and stepped onto US territory.

"Thank you, Alberto. What was that you said back there in the bar . . . before you took care of that last *pendejo*?"

"Allahu Akbar—God is great. It's Arabic. I'm Muslim. And my name is Ali, not Alberto."

The two men never discussed that night again, although it marked the beginning of relationships that endured for generations and fused the two families together in profound ways. Jack never told Marcie about the fight, and, like many dustups in the lawless towns along the Texas–Mexico frontier, nothing ever came of it. Marcie had her suspicions about the bruise on the side of Jack's face. But she never asked because she didn't want to know, and she could sense that Jack didn't want to tell her. Certain relationships between men and women—particularly in rural Texas during the 1940s and 1950s—worked that way, and worked well.

Jack and Ali were largely silent during the two-hour drive back to the farm outside Dell City. The first real words came when Jack shifted his Ford Nylint pickup into park next to one of the barracks at Camp 16.

"Look, Ali, I don't give a shit what you are. Any man who stands with me like you did back there—and for our country in the war—deserves better than what you've got."

Ali said nothing.

"There's a decent line shack on the farm, nothing fancy . . . dry, solid, and not too far from our place. It's yours for as long as you want it."

"I'm appreciative, Mr. Laws. I'll get my belongings."

"Two other things, Ali. Call me Jack, and take tomorrow off to fix the place up. Day after, come on by the house for breakfast. I want to introduce you properly to the foreman, seeing as you're his new assistant. I'm giving you a promotion and a raise. . . . Here's fifty dollars to start it off."

For the first time since before the war, Ali felt good about himself, about the future. *God is great*, he thought. *Allahu Akbar.*

Ali fit right in. He was a man of few words, but what he said was taken seriously, and the workers respected him. He was smart, took naturally to the mechanics of farming and farm equipment, and worked as long as it took to get a job done. That line shack was his first real home, and Marcie helped him fix it up with a few appliances and other niceties that a man like Ali would not have bothered with, like curtains and matching plates. The war and all those bloody, disemboweled Japanese soldiers still came back to him in dreams, but less so as the months wore on. The wounds would heal, but the scars would remain. He was okay with that and hoped his God would be too.

Marcie came by a few months later and asked Ali to drive her into El Paso for provisions. The Two T's Grocery in Dell City worked for basics, and served a pretty decent fried chicken lunch, but offered little in the way of groceries beyond Spam and toilet paper. Ali liked Marcie, felt at ease with her, and looked forward to knocking off a little early for the drive.

"I got you a little something," she said, handing Ali a bag from Starr Western Wear with a new ranger belt and a pressed white yoke shirt in it, translucent snaps for buttons that may have been authentic mother of pearl, although he wasn't certain, and it didn't matter. But Ali would sure wear it into town later in the day, with the Islamic crescent necklace his father had given him before the war underneath it.

During the shopping trip with Marcie, Ali began to remember what it was like having fun, and he liked it when she laughed, which was often but not too often. Their last stop was at Daoud's Tailor Shop, owned by a Lebanese family that had come to El Paso a generation ago, so Marcie could have a dress altered. Marcie still had her figure at forty-five, and Jack still liked it under a see-through nightie or with nothing on it at all, but a few inches had moved south on her middle due to childbearing.

That's when Ali met Sana, Daoud's oldest daughter, who had been managing the business end of the store since graduating from the University of Texas at El Paso last year. Ali had not seen many Muslim women without hijab, the traditional head covering, and Sana didn't have one on. But out of respect to her father, Sana wore her hair up in a light blue silk scarf. Marcie had been coming to Daoud's for years and had watched Sana grow into a woman of exotic beauty: thick black hair, piercing brown eyes, and a willowy grace about her that reminded Ali of a picture depicting the Queen of Sheba from a book about medieval tapestries that his mother had once shown him.

The rest of that story, as Marcie would say numerous times over the coming years and during a toast at their wedding—a blend of Muslim tradition and Texas hoedown—was "history."

Ali carried Sana across the threshold of his one-room house on their wedding night, not quite sure what would happen next. Sure, he had been with women in Juarez and in the Philippines, but those were illusions of intimacy that always ended with him putting a few dollars on the bedside table. Sana excused herself for several minutes in the bathroom, in which Jack had helped Ali install running water, a toilet, and a tub, while Ali bumbled around the kitchen. He heard the bathroom door open and turned around to find Sana standing naked in the full light of the room. It took his breath away, not only the perfection of Sana's womanhood— her breasts, the generous black hair that ran in a narrow line from her belly button to a wide triangle between her legs—but that God had given him such a gift.

"You're the first," Sana said just before Ali entered her. He was slow at the beginning, tender, and surprised at how wet she was where their bodies joined. They moved together in silent rhythm, Sana holding his face close to hers, holding it tight, and looking into his eyes—the only person in the world at that moment. He was also surprised at how many times they coupled that night and at the eruptions of passion from Sana, nothing like what he would have expected from the demure young woman he'd met that first day in her father's shop with Marcie. That passion, that secret bond between husband and wife, endured through more than four decades of marriage.

Their only child, their son, Orhan, was born a few years after Jack and Marcie had their two children, Ray and Eulalia.

CHAPTER 4

Marcie had been right. The Chihuahuan Desert was brutally hot most of the year and so dry that not much but scrub and cactus could survive without water, and plenty of it, which there was buried deep in the hundred-square-mile Bone Springs–Victorio Peak Aquifer. The aquifer was fed by the plentiful snowmelt that ran off the Sacramento Mountains, two hundred miles into New Mexico just east of Tularosa. Jack had all the water he needed for his crops, and the mercantile exchanges in Chicago and New York were awash with contracts for bales of Laws' cotton.

Jack didn't know that when he and a crew drilled their first exploratory well, hoping they might strike oil. But when they heard a gushing sound coming up the casing of the drill pipe, it was water that came flowing out by the hundreds of gallons, not crude. Jack was a little disappointed when he told Marcie about it at the supper table that evening, but the significance of what that meant for the farm was not lost on him. "We came looking for oil and found water."

But the Carter years in Washington were not good for the Laws. Under President Jimmy Carter, a peanut farmer and a Democrat, oil prices had soared from $3 to $12 a barrel due to a boycott by the Organization of Petroleum Exporting

Countries in the wake of the 1973 Yom Kippur war between Israel and its immediate Arab neighbors. Gas prices and interest rates spiked, and the price of commodities dropped through the floor. As a result, Jack was having trouble servicing the land note held by Connecticut Mutual, and he had no choice but to sell off 35,000 of what by the mid-1970s had grown to 140,000 acres and a hundred water wells. An attorney in Dallas had connected Jack to a family of wildcatters in Denver who had grown a diversified corporation out of their oil riches, and they had purchased the land at a good price. He'd also thought about chucking farming altogether in favor of the water-selling business.

But Marcie suspected the Denver group was in it for the water play. She pored over microfilmed documents at the El Paso Library and hosted her share of lunches with Texas congressmen at the Driskill Hotel a few blocks from the capitol in Austin. She found under the current law that "the right of capture" granted domain over any amount you could pump out of the ground, something very unpopular among smallholder farmers in Texas worried about the availability of water for their few acres. Although none of them alone had the grease to move the needle in Austin, together they could be a formidable force and wielded considerable political clout at the ballot box. Marcie also discovered two other important developments in all her digging: the farm bloc was pushing for new regulations that determined water rights based on actual usage over the past ten years, and El Paso was so concerned about running out of water for the growing city that some officials had been discussing the feasibility of purchasing rights from farmers in Dell City.

Jack was caught on the horns of a dilemma. He wanted to ease out of farming over the next decade or so, and selling millions of dollars of water rights to El Paso could set his family up for generations. But the amount of water he could sell would shrink to almost nothing if the regulations changed. Jack had some breathing room with the recent sale of land to the group in Denver, and Marcie advised him to bide his time and let her work the politics while the "pot simmered." Neither of them had any idea then just how explosive the issue would become. But they began to sense it in the aftermath of a story Andrew Solomons wrote about the whole issue in the *Hudspeth County Herald*.

Jack slid the newspaper over the kitchen table to Marcie.

"Did you read this? Does Solomons think he's working for the *New York Times*? And what the hell is this new anonymous column, 'Burr under My Saddle?'"

"Easy, Jack. Before this is all over, it probably *will* be in the *New York Times* or the *Wall Street Journal*, certainly the *Austin American Statesman* and the El Paso papers. Just leave that part to me. And that column is a good thing—gives people a chance to vent."

"Never should have hired that Yankee Jew."

"Jack!"

CHAPTER 5

Jack's son, Ray, was one of those teenagers who sprouted hair on his privates before any of his peers, and at sixteen he was roaming around town like some wild-eyed cur sniffing for poontang. He wasn't a bad kid, at least not yet, a decent student and a good ballplayer when his mind was on something besides girls. He was Marcie's first, and she had a warm spot in her heart for him that no amount of shenanigans could take away. She'd patch him up after fights and send him on his way. Boys will be boys.

Eulalia, Eula as they called her, was a different story, sort of the flip side of Ray, and she didn't get along very well with Marcie. She was a Dell City cowgirl through and through, but she had a natural sophistication far beyond her years and never seemed to get caught: not in the barn spinning the bottle with her older friends, not behind the cotton gin smoking cigarettes, and not at the bar in the Sheepherder's drinking a beer with some blue-eyed cowboy. She was sixteen going on twenty-five and couldn't wait to put Dell City in her rearview mirror. She was also a gifted musician, with a pitch-perfect voice that Jack never tired of, and Eula imagined that could be her ticket out of the desert.

Ali's son, Orhan, a few years younger but a head taller and twenty pounds heavier than Ray, tagged along during the early years, always willing to play the Indian to his cowboy. He understood the family dynamic from the start, in part because of the stories he overheard when Jack and Ali were having a late-night chat on the porch outside his window, and he fell quickly into the role of arbiter, diplomat, and protector. Orhan might have been able to divert the train wreck barreling toward Ray late that spring evening if he hadn't been with Ali in the fields learning the trade that would be his avocation for the next fifty years.

Condoms were hard to come by in Dell City—certainly not available at the Two T's Grocery, where Patsy Cline's "Walkin' After Midnight" or Marty Robbins's "El Paso" seemed to play every hour—but Ray had been carrying one in his wallet for two years just in case he got lucky or managed to sneak down to the Mariscal, the seedy red-light district in Juarez. Getting lucky was exactly what was on his mind as he drove the faded Chevy 3100 pickup out of town on Broadway Street heading toward the turnoff for Camp 16. Jack had asked Ray to stop by Perry's Hardware for some odds and ends, but halfway there he'd felt that tightness between his legs and figured he'd just take a quick swing out of town. About a half mile out, Ray pulled over and offered two teenage girls a lift to wherever they were headed. They were redneck-white and clearly not the kind of girls Ray went to school with at Dell City High, who knew enough not to get into exactly this kind of situation with him.

"Where you headed?"

"Camp 16."

"Jump in; I'll give you a ride."

The blonde took him up on the offer, but the brunette did not. "I've got to tote these groceries home."

She was mightily impressed with Ray as he toured her around the farm, and predictably, they ended up inside an empty grain silo in the middle of nowhere. It didn't take long, but when Ray pulled out of her, the condom didn't come with him. Four months later there was a knock on Marcie's front door, and when she opened it, the blonde was standing there, clearly with child.

"Mrs. Laws."

"Yes."

"I'm Glyda Mae Pope. I live out at the camp, and my daddy works for you."

"Ray."

"I don't know what to do."

This was delicate and could not be dismissed as "boys will be boys." Marcie teased the whole story out of Ray that night and left him hanging for a long, sleepless night of imagining marriage at seventeen, with nothing but work and kids in Dell City for the next sixty years or so. No frat house at the University of Texas a few years down the road.

She discussed it with Jack, and they decided Marcie would take Glyda Mae to Juarez for an abortion, providing her family was willing.

"Her daddy is a good man, hard worker."

"But she's so young, Jack, and we're talking about a life."

Jack was pragmatic and could be cold. "Nothing a few hundred dollars and a promotion for her old man won't take care of."

"Jack."

"Marcie, Ray is not marrying some knocked-up redneck, and we're not raising that child. Not happening."

Although Marcie didn't entirely agree, this was one time when there was no room for any type of maneuvering with Jack. Marcie took Glyda Mae to a doctor in Juarez who was accustomed to exactly this type of situation and, for $125, took care of it in less than an hour. Marcie held her hand every second of the procedure and never forgot the look on Glyda

Mae Pope's face as she dropped her off at Camp 16. Helpless, tossed by powers she would never understand. Marcie tried to pray that night but couldn't find the words. She was hiding the truth, unclean and unworthy of forgiveness.

Dell City High School wasn't right for Eula. There was no music program to mention except what passed for a band that didn't do much more than play the national anthem at football games, and she'd been going to the hoity-toity Radford School in the Austin Heights neighborhood of El Paso since ninth grade. That's where she really learned to play the guitar and sing a cappella. Radford was a world away from Dell City, and all the students there—many of whom would go on to careers in law, medicine, government, oil, or a prosperous family real estate development company—were every bit as clever as she.

A few days before Ray and Orhan were to pick her up for Christmas break, Eula overheard a conversation between two of her girlfriends in which one of them referred to her as "quaint." That really stuck in Eula's craw, so much so that she convinced Ray and Orhan to take a side trip to Juarez before heading back to Dell City. "I'll show them fucking quaint."

Orhan drove the pickup since he was Muslim and didn't drink. Ray and Eula had polished off a six pack of Lone Star before they parked on Calle Constitucion in front of the El Tragadero steakhouse for racks of tender beef ribs and frozen mugs of Bohemia. They marveled at old black-and-white photographs of famous matadors in blood-stained *traje de luces*, dancing inches away from charging fifteen-hundred-pound bulls as they performed a *tanda* with the *muleta*, or hovered over the massive horns, plunging a sword into the bull's heart.

The three of them cruised a few more bars before a final nightcap at the "world-famous" Kentucky Club on Avenida Benito Juarez. Ray was flat drunk, and Eula was not far behind, flirting with just about anything in a pair of pants: flipping her blond hair, swirling around the bar, touching everyone in a way that would have been harmless with the boys at a Radford School dance but that sent dangerous signals to grown Mexican men. Orhan needed to get them out of there quickly and told Eula he was taking Ray to the truck.

"Don't move. I'll be right back."

"Okay, don't worry. I just need to make a pit stop."

Looking back on that moment for the rest of his life, Orhan could never forgive himself.

Eula had to pee, and she wasn't about to squat over the trough that ran under the entire length of the bar and had been installed at the Kentucky for that exact reason, or so some drunk didn't puke on the floor. Three men were waiting for her when she emerged from the ladies' room, two big ones in their forties and one not much older than she. The two older men grabbed handfuls of her blond hair and dragged her out the back door, while the younger one followed. It happened quickly. The older ones threw her down into a puddle next to a stinking trashcan, ripping off her boots, pants, and green panties—Radford colors. One of them held her down while the other one straddled her, facing backward, and spread her legs wide as if he was neutering an animal. Eula would always remember their strength, their callused hands, the words of the man holding her down, and the look on the face of the younger one, the one who was about her age, that seemed to say, "I'm sorry, I have no choice."

"Fuck the bitch, *rapido*."

Orhan found Eula just as they had left her in that puddle by the trash. He had never seen a naked woman before. He was consumed by a fire that burned out all the innocence of his youth, and knew for the first time that he could kill. Three men in a black pickup drove slowly by as if to taunt him, and Orhan saw their faces clearly, as well as their license plate: Ciudad Juarez 82-53. One of them, the one with the scar over his eye, smiled and extended his middle finger. Orhan didn't know what to do, and he couldn't leave Eula in the alley. He should never have left her alone, drunk in that bar. Orhan helped her dress and carried her gently around the block to the truck. Eula buried her face in the crook of his neck and sobbed.

It didn't take but a few days after Eula came home for Jack to pay off the right people in Juarez for those bastards' address, and to convince the police to look the other way. Jack had stowed the sawed-off and the scoped 45.70 in the back seat of the truck. Ali had tucked the old army trench knife into his right boot. They had both killed and knew there would be blood that night.

They pulled the truck behind the house in the Lomas Del Rey neighborhood near the airfield. It was the middle of the night, but they could see the three of them smoking on the back porch. Ali used the binoculars to verify that there were two older men, one with a scar over his eye, and a third who looked to be about seventeen.

Jack went to the car and pulled out the 45.70, a powerful bear gun that he'd used to drop a six-hundred-pound grizzly in its tracks from a hundred yards on a hunting trip to Montana. He propped it on the fence behind the house and shot the one with the scar square in the face, a simple target from no more than twenty-five yards that took off most of his head. Ali had slipped around the bushes behind them. A second after Jack shot, he whispered, "Allahu Akbar," and, quick as a cat, yanked the other one's head back, cutting his throat to the spine. The sound of blood spewing from the jugular brought the war and those fights with the Japanese in the jungle back to him. Jack held the sawed-off in both hands as he strode across the grass to the young one, the angel of death come to collect his due. Ali felt sorry for the kid, until he remembered how Eula had looked that night at the kitchen table when they all returned from Juarez. Jack looked him square in the eyes and lowered the 12-gauge about two feet, and Ali thought his friend might show mercy. Then Jack emptied both barrels into the kid's groin. He probably wouldn't survive, and he wouldn't be doing any more raping if he did.

CHAPTER 6

It's not easy being a Muslim in West Texas, particularly when you're a football-playing Muslim during August two-a-day workouts that fall during Ramadan, a month of fasting that commemorates the first revelation of the Qur'an to the Prophet Muhammad. Crockett Laws and Tamerlane Zarkan, Ray and Orhan's only sons, had grown used to it ever since they'd first snapped on football helmets as ragtag fifth graders at Dell City Elementary to begin a rite of passage in Texas that has defined the lives of men from Amarillo to Brownsville.

Coach Billy Tarnowski, Coach T, started practice at dawn Sunday morning, which gave the Cougars a few hours of tolerable weather before the sun climbed over the Guadalupe Mountains that surround Dell City and the temperature began creeping north of a hundred degrees. But that barely gave Tamerlane time before sunrise to load up with enough food and water to carry him through the twelve-hour fast his faith and his parents required.

"Blood Alley, gentlemen," Coach T barked, one last hitting drill before summer practices ended. "Get some water and line up."

Crockett Laws was a rangy six-footer who tipped the scale at about 190 and could rip a football forty yards on the run with the kind of precision and mechanics that had not gone unnoticed by college scouts. Crockett picked up his helmet and walked to the water cooler on the sideline, a puff of dust with every step. Keeping your helmet with you at all times, like a soldier with his rifle, was one of those details that Coach T hammered into them, one of those details that separates good teams from great ones. Crockett and Tam knew full well that a drink was not in the cards for any observant Muslim in the world as long as the sun was still up. He admired Tam—loved him, really, in the way of comrades in the trenches of a great endeavor. Their grandfathers, Jack and Ali, and their fathers, Ray and Orhan, had forged the same kind of bond through generations of farming and living in this tiny West Texas community. Tam rested his forehead on the side of the aluminum water cooler, and Crockett poured a scoop of ice down his friend's neck, about the size and density of a blowout preventer on one of those oil derricks along the endless highways that cut through the high desert of West Texas. Tam smiled, that same whimsical smile Crockett knew from those dinners when Mrs. Zarkan gave him a second helping of chile rellenos casserole "Syrian style," with succulent chunks of spicy lamb under the cornmeal-breaded fried chilies.

Texas produces football legends: Slinging Sammy Baugh, who twice led the Washington Redskins to an NFL championship; Bobby Layne, who quarterbacked the Detroit Lions to three; Dick "Night Train" Lane; the Dallas Cowboy immortal Bob Lilly; Mean Joe Green; and Earl Campbell, to name a few enshrined in the NFL Hall of Fame. And West Texas seemed to breed more than its share.

But they all played traditional eleven-man ball, many at the perennial powerhouse rivals, Odessa Permian and Midland Lee. Crockett and Tam played in a six-man league against teams from nearby towns like Fort Davis, Sierra Blanca, and Marfa, none of which had enough students to field an eleven-man squad. It's a fast game, but no less violent or less skilled, that favors endurance quickness and guile. "You got to run like a deer," Coach T would say. "Run all day." Crockett and Tam were outliers in six-man, with the size and talent to have starred on any team in Texas. They were men among boys with most opponents, and Andrew Solomons had written a preseason story in the *Hudspeth County Herald* picking the Cougars as the favorite to win the league championship—headlined "Laying Down The Law(s)."

The Cougars had been running like deer during this entire two-hour practice, finishing up with Blood Alley. "Assume the position, gentlemen," Coach T said, and thirteen players split up to form the alley down which two would run headfirst at each other from a few yards away—one ballcarrier, one tackler. Tam always went first, coiling into a three-point stance like one of the rattlesnakes that could strike from under almost any rock in the high desert. Crockett had lined up against Tam on many occasions, and slipped by him on a few, but he'd been dealt his share of ferocious hits too. On this particular day, he was grateful that Coach T would not allow his starting quarterback to participate. Javier Shirley, a prototype six-man player with good hands and quick feet who was Crockett's favorite receiver, scooped up the ball and ambled into the alley opposite Tam in a way that might give him the jump on an unsuspecting opponent. But the physics were not in his favor. "On the whistle," Coach T said, and a few seconds later, Javier seemed to explode, ball one way and body the other. Tam liked Javier and respected all his opponents. In some ways, he regretted the pounding he often dealt them, but he also craved that feeling when the full energy of his 230 pounds transferred into an opponent like a lightning strike on a tree. Crockett could only shake his head at the predictable outcome of this mismatch and smile as Tam sheepishly offered a hand-up to Javier.

After a few more rounds, Coach T ended it, and all that remained of summer practice was the traditional midnight scrimmage in a few hours.

CHAPTER 7

Sunday night dinner was always a big deal for the Laws, who called it a barbecue, and for the Zarkans, who, during Ramadan, called it iftar, the daily breaking of the dawn-to-dusk fast that is among the most revered rituals in Islam.

Three generations of Laws lived outside of town surrounded by 150,000 acres of cotton, long green chilies, oats, onions, tomatoes, barley, and cantaloupes—most of it cotton. Jack and Marcelina lived in a sprawling two-story ranch house, with an outside firepit large enough to barbecue a steer. Ray; his son, Crockett; and his wife, Bitsy, a Dallas gal who had never quite adjusted to life without Neiman Marcus, lived in a faux-colonial farmhouse about a mile away. And Eula lived alone in a funky line shack that would not have seemed out of place tucked into the craggy cliffs of Big Sur.

Their pickups surrounded the firepit like a wagon train bracing for a Comanche attack, and Ray, five Lone Stars into the early evening, threw another mesquite log on the coals. Marcie, calico apron hugging sixty-four-year-old hips that didn't look half bad doing the Cotton-Eyed Joe at the Bronco Dancehall in El Paso, flipped the steaks. Bitsy was nursing a vodka, neat, while Eula played guitar and Crockett thought about the scrimmage, his girlfriend Lola Mae, and where he'd be this time next year.

Crockett had a drawer full of form letters from college programs and had been visited by coaches from two scrappy Division III teams: Sul Ross State, 190 miles south in Alpine, and Hardin Simmons, six hours east in Abilene. The University of Texas coach had invited him to walk on, as had the coach at Texas A&M. But it was the call from the Army Black Knights' coach at West Point a few months earlier that had most impressed him. The Hudson River Valley was worlds away from Dell City and Lola Mae, but West Point, an officer's commission, and the chance to lead men into battle overseas appealed to something innocent in him that had not yet been touched by the cold reality of war. The words from the West Point coach stuck with him: "It's not for everybody, Crockett, but I think it's for you. You'll hate it most of the time, but you'll love it enough." And the coach had invited him to visit later in the year, a trip for which Bitsy was already laying out her ensemble.

"I'll be like Douglas MacArthur's mother," Bitsy said—again.

Eula stopped playing the guitar and rolled her eyes. "No, Bitsy, you won't be like fucking MacArthur's mom."

"Eula." Marcie sighed. "Please."

Ray cracked another Lone Star.

Mary Pinkney Hardy MacArthur was the woman of substance and lineage that Bitsy thought she might have been had she not married Ray after graduating from the University of Texas and moved to godforsaken Dell City—in her mind like Elizabeth Taylor in *Giant*, but in reality more akin to Eva Gabor in that goofy 1960s sitcom *Green Acres*. Mary MacArthur was the daughter of a prominent North Carolina businessman and the wife of Arthur MacArthur Jr., a Union general who received the Medal of Honor for heroism during the Battle of Missionary Ridge near Chattanooga, Tennessee. To say she was overbearing with her beloved son, Douglas, would have been an understatement of historic proportions. She was so fixated on Douglas's success that she moved into the Thayer Hotel on the grounds of West Point when her son attended, occupying a suite facing his dormitory room in Central Area in order to monitor his study habits.

West Point admission requires a formal nomination from a congressman or certain other officials, even if you're a five-star recruit with an arm like a cannon. Jack Laws had connections, plenty of them, that helped on behalf of his grandson. He had manned the .50-caliber on a World War II amphibious gunboat with Texas Senator John Tower and lost his right thumb during an assault on the island of Sausapor in Western New Guinea. Jack and the senator had stayed in touch over the years, and Tower was happy to provide Crockett the congressional nomination required for admission.

"What are you thinking," Jack asked Crockett.

"West Point, Abuelo." That's what the kids called Jack, Spanish for grandfather.

"It's free," Ray said. "Two hundred fifty K worth of free."

"I know, Dad."

"Free, huh," Marcelina said with a hint of sarcasm, looking a few years down the road to a cold gravestone in some military cemetery with Crockett six feet under it.

Marcie was as patriotic as the next person, but she had lived through the body counts of Vietnam and the onslaught of Pentagon propaganda that had brainwashed two generations of American youth into thinking that war would be like some movie where the Navy Seals kiss their sleepy, foxy blond wives and kids goodbye in San Diego, jump out of a plane at night, blow up some Arabs or Mexican drug dealers, and return to a boozy celebration in a homey rural bar where the owner has pictures of them on the wall surfing. She'd had enough of the bullshit: country music, video games, F-16s flying over the Super Bowl. She looked at Crockett, her beautiful Crockett. Eula, rebel without a pause, said what Marcie was thinking.

"If you die, I'll kill you."

Meanwhile, a few miles away on the fringes of the Laws' farm, not far from Camp 16, where migrant workers lived during the harvest, the Zarkans were preparing for their first meal since predawn breakfast. The family carried their obligation with dignity and without complaint, but at this point in the day during Ramadan, they all looked as if they'd been locked for hours in a car with the windows rolled up on a hot day.

As the matriarch at fifty-eight, Sana presided over the pots of chicken, lamb, lentils, and rice. The pungent aroma from pots of rice, saffron, and harissa floated into the backyard, where her husband, Ali, the foreman on the Laws' farm; Orhan, his son and assistant; and Tam sat patiently waiting for the sun to drop behind the Otero Mesa. Orhan's wife, Bernia, the most devout of the group, kept her mind off of her hunger and thirst by reciting under her breath the prayer that ends each day's fast: "O Allah! I fasted for You and I believe in You and I put my trust in You and I break my fast with your sustenance."

The Zarkans were legendary wrestlers going way back in Syria, and grappling was an affectionate family bonding ritual that could break out at a moment's notice. Ali shouted, "Zarkan wrestling," and threw his trademark headlock around Tam's bull neck. Tam, completely depleted after a two-hour practice and the daily fast, pretended to struggle, but in reality he barely had enough strength to slip from his grandfather's arms, leathery and roped from decades of farm work. The three men fell into a joyous heap, all flopping arms and legs like a bunch of puppies scrambling for milk. It didn't last long, mostly because Tam didn't want any inadvertent sprains or bruises before midnight scrimmage.

"That coach from UTEP called last week," said Tam,

referring to the University of Texas at El Paso, a big-time Division I program that had sent its share of players to the NFL, like Jets' Hall of Fame receiver Don Maynard in the mid-fifties.

"Yeah," Orhan said.

"I'm a six-man guy, so probably no money until I prove it. But he may invite me to walk on, and he said he believes in me."

"What did you say?"

"Well, I'm not going to West Point like Crockett. So I told him probably yes."

"You will make it, Inshallah," said Ali. God willing.

After dinner, both families made their way to Dell City High School for the midnight scrimmage. Jack sat next to his friend and foreman Ali, Ray beside Orhan, and all the women a row below, appealing to whatever God they believed in that Tam and Crockett both avoid injury. Everyone pretended that Ray didn't smell like a distillery, something particularly obvious to the Zarkans, who, like all observant Muslims, did not drink.

Crockett's longtime girlfriend, Lola Mae Kincaid, and her younger sister, Lola Beth, bounced and cartwheeled around with the other three cheerleaders in front of the stands, the kind of buxom country girls that artsy types referred to as Rubenesque and rednecks referred to as "built like a brick shithouse." The Kincaid sisters would never have imagined the thoughts crossing the minds of more than a few old boys in the stands, and they might have worn sports bras if they did. Crockett was very fond of that particular part of Lola Mae. But he respected her too, and like the gentleman he had been raised to be, he didn't push her any further than the God she believed in was prepared to forgive before marriage. Tam nudged Crockett in the ribs on the bench when he caught him paying more attention to Lola Mae's bouncing around than to the game.

The Fort Davis Indians were no match for the Cougars, and Coach T pulled Crockett and Tam from the game after the first two scrimmage series of ten plays, but not before Crockett ran for two touchdowns and hit Javier for three. Tam made mincemeat of the Indians' quarterback, sacking him five times and causing three fumbles, one of which he recovered and ran for a score.

CHAPTER 8

The Cougars' first game of the 1984 season was Saturday night against the Sierra Blanca Vaqueros, and Jack picked Crockett up just before dawn for opening day of deer hunting season. A good friend had given them the keys to the gates at Rancho Seco, an eight-hundred-acre spread twenty miles west of Dell City at the base of the Guadalupe Mountains. And Jack was taking his grandson there for what would probably be his last chance to bag his first deer before going off to college.

They pulled through the last gate and parked next to the pavilion, a simple wooden structure that his friends had been tinkering with for years. It was perfect for a few nights of beer drinking next to the firepit for the hearty crowd, and even bearable for the more well-heeled visitors from Dallas or Houston, particularly since they had added a propane-heated shower and fashioned a sit-down toilet by screwing a seat on the kind of four-legged walker hobbled folks used to get around.

Jack pulled his old Marlin lever-action 30.30 out of the faded leather scabbard, a collectors' item worth a few thousand dollars that could still shoot like the first day out of the box, and handed it to Crockett.

"This here's your graduation gift, son."

"Abuelo, the thirty . . . !"

"The scabbard too."

Thanks seemed puny for the occasion, and Crockett simply hugged his seventy-year-old granddad, who was unaccustomed to such displays of affection but returned it in a way that left no doubt about the depth of his feelings.

They walked past the fences surrounding the pistachio trees, in which their friends had rigged a solar-powered drip-irrigation system, and headed up the mountain before the sun rose and the swirling wind picked up enough scent to spook any waking deer. They settled in a notch between some rocks halfway up and waited for signs. Jack peered through the binoculars, the ones Ali had used on that violent night in Juarez so many years ago, and wondered whether Crockett would ever face such perils. Certainly he would if West Point was his choice.

"Crockett, seventy yards to the right . . . next to that pile of rocks . . . a ten-point buck waiting for a bullet."

Crockett engaged the lever, and the deer froze at the click of a 30 mm shell dropping into the chamber. As Jack had taught him, Crockett propped his elbows on his knees to steady the gun and took a few easy breaths, holding the last exhale as he stared down the barrel through the iron sights. The deer fell a few seconds after Crockett pulled the trigger, and didn't move.

They walked over to the buck, and Jack dipped a finger into blood from the wound where the bullet had shattered his shoulder and pierced his heart, smearing a little on Crockett's forehead. First blood, a tradition as old as hunting. They gutted the deer, skinned it, and lugged what was left—which Marcie would butcher into venison steaks and sausage—back to the truck.

Tamerlane's morning was a little different, starting with his routine before every game the past three years: Fajr, the

Muslim dawn prayer, then a big breakfast, followed by a few hours sitting with Sana and Bernia while they knitted and spoke in Arabic about whatever struck them. At these times, it was hard for the two women to imagine Tam as the marauding linebacker so feared by his opponents.

The gentle clicking of the knitting needles, the ancient rhythms of Arabic, and their laughter soothed Tam before combat, somehow prepared him for the battle ahead—as if he needed his cup of decency filled before he could morph into the most feared six-man linebacker west of Abilene. And the Cougars would need every inch of his inner goblin to beat the Vaqueros, who had taken a squeaker from them last year in the six-man championship at the Alamodome in San Antonio.

CHAPTER 9

HUDSPETH COUNTY HERALD

COUGARS SLASH THE VAQUEROS

By Andrew Solomons

DELL CITY_Fueled by the arm of Crockett Laws and the grit of Tamerlane Zarkan, the Cougars avenged their heartbreaking loss to the Vaqueros in the state finals last year with a stunning come-from-behind 35-27 victory over Sierra Blanca Saturday night.

Uncharacteristically, the Cougars came out flat, with a seemingly sluggish Laws unable to move the ball in the first half. They weren't much better on defense, even though Zarkan, prowling sideline to sideline, accounted for 12 tackles and two sacks on Vaqueros quarterback Mordecai Stevenson.

But Zarkan couldn't do it alone, and Stevenson, who amassed 200 yards in the air and 40 on the ground, had the Vaqueros up 24-0 at halftime.

Following a tongue-lashing from Coach T at halftime—which one player, who asked not to be named, characterized as him "throwing everything at us but the kitchen sink"—the Cougars came out on fire.

Laws marched the Cougars down the field after the opening kickoff, completing four consecutive passes, the last one a 38-yard strike to Javier Shirley in the corner of the end zone. Zarkan, hobbled by a twisted knee, separated the Vaquero return man from the ball with a bone-crushing hit on the ensuing kickoff and rumbled into the end zone to make it 24-14.

The Cougar squad continued the thrilling comeback on both sides of the ball, with Laws firing bullets all over the field, at one point in the fourth quarter breaking the Texas six-man record for consecutive completions with 27 straight. Zarkan was relentless, accounting for all but 10 of the Cougars' stops on defense, holding the Vaqueros to a single field goal late in the third quarter.

The Cougars went up by a point on a breathtaking 70-yard punt return by Shirley with 10 minutes remaining in the fourth quarter. And Laws delivered the coup de grace on the Cougars' final possession, running it in from the Vaqueros 30.

The Cougars are away next Saturday against the Fort Davis Indians.

CHAPTER 10

Nobody was any more thrilled to be at West Point than Bitsy Laws. The head coach, whose Black Knights appeared headed to a bowl game for the first time in the ninety-four years they had been fielding a team, had invited Crockett for an official visit. And Bitsy had been preparing for months.

She'd spent hours prowling Neiman Marcus at Northpark Mall in Dallas, on the fringes of her beloved Highland Park, the uber-elite neighborhood where she had grown up a few blocks from the WASP-only Dallas Country Club. Bitsy's mother was not far off the truth when she joked about being buried under the inlaid tile entrance to the store to ensure her daughter would visit the grave. But her mother was the last thing on Bitsy's mind as she interrogated makeup, hair, and fashion consultants on colors, lengths, and attire for the two-day visit to Highland Falls in late October. Bitsy tried to restrain herself with the shop girls, who would probably never travel any farther north than Denton, but pettiness bred in the lonely desert of West Texas over the past twenty years was too much to suppress, and she made sure anyone within earshot knew that Bitsy Laws was going places. *Those dummies have probably never even heard of West Point*, Bitsy thought smugly as she sashayed through the aisles of the store.

A midcalf tartan plaid skirt and a simple white Oxford-cloth shirt under a luxurious, but understated, tan V-neck cashmere sweater would be perfect for the eighty-minute train ride from Penn Station to Garrison, New York, just across the Hudson River from Highland Falls and West Point. The fall weather could be erratic in upstate New York, and Bitsy was prepared; a new jaunty "West Point gray" beret was tucked in her tan Longchamp bag, with a full-length faux Burberry trench coat slung through the loops, and a shiny new pair of dark blue Sperry Top-Siders were on her feet. They were just like the ones she used to slip on at the Pi Phi house before heading to a kegger at SAE with her future husband, Ray, on a rainy football weekend at the University of Texas. She had bought Crockett a matching pair of Top-Siders, in light nubuck, but he wore his best pair of brown leather cowboy boots instead.

"Nothing about Douglas MacArthur's mother, okay, Mom?"

"Oh, Crockett."

The head coach came to the train station to meet them with the offensive and defensive captains, fresh off a 48-13 win against Penn to bring their record to 4-1-1, the most promising start for the Black Knights in more than a decade. The coach, a consummate gentleman, opened the car door for Bitsy, and she racked her brain to recall whether Ray had ever done that for her in the twenty-three years she'd known him. Crockett and his Cougars were 8-0 after a victory against the Grandfalls-Royalty Cowboys, and as soon as they began the drive to campus, the coach commented on another stellar offensive day for Crockett.

"I've recruited a few six-man ballplayers, Crockett. Sets you up well for our brand of football. We don't have a lot of time to practice fancy formations or complicated passing schemes. As a matter of fact, with all the other demands on a

cadet . . . military, academic . . . we usually practice just three
times a week during the season. It's old school here—run the
rock, option, boot, hit somebody."

Crockett, who was a little insecure about his pedigree as
a six-man player graduating into an eleven-man D1 program,
liked the sound of it. Bitsy wasn't sure what the coach meant,
but she sure thought the touch of gray on his sideburns was
distinguished.

They stopped at the historic Thayer Hotel, just inside the
West Point gates, for Bitsy and Crockett to check into their
rooms, and Bitsy thought she'd "died and gone to heaven" when
the bellhop escorted them to the Douglas MacArthur suite.

They drove around Lusk Reservoir and by historic Michie
Stadium, which thrilled Crockett as much as the MacArthur
suite had thrilled Bitsy, on their way to Trophy Point overlooking the Hudson River Valley in its full autumn glory.
The tour was like a living illustration of Crockett's American
history textbook: the plain where George Washington and
his troops camped during the Revolutionary War; the battle
monument to the Civil War—an ornate Tuscan pillar with
cannons buried muzzle first around it to symbolize peace in a
unified nation; and the cavernous multifaith Cadet's Chapel
with its more than twenty thousand organ pipes. Crockett
could feel the immensity of history as they overlooked the
Hudson River from the tip of Trophy Point, and Coach Young
explained the engineering behind the Great Chain—sixty-five
tons of locally forged interlocking steel stretched six hundred
yards across the river to stop British ships during the Revolutionary War.

They arrived for lunch at Grant Hall as all four thousand
cadets were lining up outside, just as they did three times a day
every day for meals that lasted exactly forty minutes. Crockett
tried to imagine himself as a first-year plebe, serving family
style to his table of "yearlings, cows, and firsties," each of

them demanding under threat of punishment that he recite the menu from memory and recall all of their dining preferences, right down to the number of ice cubes in their drinks.

Crockett's head was spinning as he lay in bed that night at the Thayer Hotel. The coach had formally offered him a spot on the team as a recruit and informally told him that his grades, SAT scores, and nomination from Senator John Tower had passed muster with the admission committee. There was an awkward silence in the coach's office after he made the offer, the only sound the impatient chafing of Bitsy's hose as she uncrossed and crossed her legs. No question what she wanted, but Marcie's deep misgivings as well as doubts about what would become of his relationship with Lola Mae crept in. And Tam.

More than two thousand miles away, Tam was in the UTEP football weight room with the head coach, in the midst of a dismal season for the Miners. Tam was mesmerized as he watched Seth Joyner, a linebacker about his size who would go on to an NFL career that included three all-pro selections and a Super Bowl ring with the Denver Broncos, power-clean almost 350 pounds, four sets of five reps in eight minutes. "When Doves Cry" by Prince blasted out of the speakers, followed by Bruce Springsteen's "Born in the USA." Tam dug it but would have preferred something from Alabama or the Nitty Gritty Dirt Band.

Tam didn't really click with the head coach, who, with his big ears, obvious toupee, and gut spilling over double-knit coaching shorts, looked more like a goofy plumber or a NASCAR functionary than a D1 coach. He'd spent most of his career on the football fields of West Texas, most recently at West Texas A&M, and you could cut his drawl with a dull butter knife. But the defensive coordinator and linebacker coach was a different story. He had an easy way with the players, and Joyner clearly respected him.

The defensive coordinator, accompanied by his student assistant, an attractive young Latina with a clipboard, walked Tam through the Durham Sports Center, pointing out the rooms where each position group met to review film or go over game plans. The halls were lined with photographs of renowned former players, like Fred Carr and Hall of Famer Don Maynard. The coach pointed to the sign on the door of the tight ends' meeting room, which doubled as the NFL scouting room.

"Tom Landry was in there last week; Dan Reeves the week before."

The three of them sat down in cramped classroom chairs with small, oval-shaped desktops attached, and Tam could barely fit without scrunching his size-twelve feet under the notebook basket below the seat.

"I like your film, Tam. You're fun to watch, a local boy and a Mexican—excuse me, an American of Mexican descent. If it were up to me, which it's not, I'd give you a full ride. But our head coach has a few other linebackers coming out of eleven-man schools—Odessa Permian, Houston Strake Jesuit, and Austin Southlake Carroll. We want you as a preferred walk-on. You'll get as good a look as any of them and a scholarship your next year if you're as good as I think you are."

"I'm not a Mexican American, coach. I'm an American, Syrian heritage. Muslim."

The coach shifted uneasily, and his student assistant, the brown-skinned girl who had clearly been included in the tour to emphasize diversity, dropped her eyes to the clipboard. Tam looked the coach in the eye, as Orhan and Ali had taught him, and chuckled in that inclusive way that puts people at ease in an otherwise awkward situation.

"No worries, coach. Happens all the time. I appreciate the chance. You'll see. I'm not the type to let an opportunity slip by. I'm looking at Sul Ross and a few other schools. I'll have to talk with my family."

"Fair enough, Tam. It's yours if you want it. Olivia will give you some paperwork, take you around campus, and you'll be getting some mail about next steps. Good luck to you, and to that nifty QB Crockett Laws, with the rest of the season."

Tam was no stranger to UTEP, having served as the designated driver for Crockett and their friends on many a night of beer crawls after a Saturday afternoon Miners game. But he had never visited the Interfaith Center, which Olivia walked him through in what Tam felt was an attempt to make amends for the coach's blunder about his being a Mexican. He didn't mention the absence of a Qur'an or any other symbol of Islam. The football cafeteria was impressive, but tray after tray of sizzling pork was a definite turnoff.

Tam drove the long way up Mesa to I-10 so he could stop by the small mosque on Paragon Lane. He performed the afternoon prayer, Asr, facing east along with a handful of Muslim men of all colors and nationalities, each one reciting softly to himself the words of a faith that stretches back centuries while he alternately leaned forward or bent to his knees as the ritual required.

"In the name of Allah, the infinitely compassionate and merciful . . . Glory to Allah, the exalted . . . Oh, Allah, forgive me and my parents. . . . Glory to Allah, the most high."

Tam paid his respects to Orhan's friend, the assistant imam, on his way out and noticed a girl about his age who had just prayed in a separate room with the other women. She was clearly observant—conservative dress, but a light blue scarf rather than hijab—and Tam felt a connection to her beyond religion and geography. The assistant imam could not help but notice and introduced him to Almira Hamzeh, the daughter of a successful Lebanese businessman in El Paso, captain of the tennis team at Radford with plans to attend UTEP next fall.

"Women's studies."

"Ag and football."

"Muslim footballer. That should be interesting."

"Maybe we could . . ."

"See each other next year? I hope so."

Tam was not big on small talk, especially with girls he didn't know, and after a few awkward seconds, they parted. But at that moment, Tam no longer had any question about which college he would attend.

CHAPTER 11

Tam knew his right wrist was broken and dislocated the second a Jayton Jayhawks lineman had stomped it under a pile and he'd heard a snap. Like a jolt of electricity, the pain shot up his arm, and Tam felt like puking when he looked at the wrist pointing unnaturally at a right angle, the tip of a jagged yellow bone poking through the skin. Blood dripped on Javier's white cleats in the huddle, and he leaned back to retch. The referee called an official timeout, with forty-eight seconds remaining on the clock at the Alamodome in San Antonio, Jayhawks three points up and deep in Cougars territory during the fourth quarter of the state six-man championship.

Coach T met Tam halfway to the sideline and held his linebacker's massive arm at the elbow on the way to the Cougars' bench. Doc Alvarado had seen his share of grisly rural accidents, but nothing quite like this in a decade of doctoring at football games. Crockett wrapped an arm around Tam's shoulder pads as he leaned in to see and to support his best friend. The doctor shook his head.

"You're done."

The last moments of his high school career, and Tam wasn't having any of that.

"Wrap it. Forty-eight seconds to glory."

Tam recited to himself the Muslim Dua through the pain as the doctor yanked the bone into place and wrapped white athletic tape around his wrist until it looked like some kind of bloody club. "In the name of Allah the compassionate and merciful. I seek refuge with Allah and His omnipotence from the evil of what I feel and that which I am wary of."

The entire Laws and Zarkan clans had traveled together to San Antonio in a rented RV for the game—Jack, Marcie, Ray, Bitsy, Eula, Ali, Sana, Orhan, and Bernia—and they jumped to their feet as Tam trotted to the defensive huddle. Tam called the play, "twenty-three slam," an all-out blitz with him clearing a lane to the Jayhawks quarterback by bull-rushing the lineman who had stomped his wrist.

The Jayhawks right tackle clearly felt no remorse as he leaned into a three-point stance, mouthing "fuck you" to Tam when he looked up before the snap. Tam had noticed a tendency in the center to tap a heel just before snapping the ball, and he'd been waiting for just the right moment to take advantage of it. Tam was into the line as the ball hit the quarterback's hands, and pancaked the tackle before he knew what hit him. Javier, quick as a jackrabbit, flew through the hole and slapped the ball high into the air. It hung suspended for what seemed like a moment frozen in time, two thousand pairs of eyes fixed on a single point of history. The ball dropped miraculously to Tam, who snagged it with his one good hand in what would become known over the years in Dell City lore as "The Catch."

Thirty-two seconds, two plays, and sixty yards later, Crockett stepped into the Jayhawks' end zone on a quarterback boot, and the Cougars were state champions.

Andrew Solomons stayed up all night to push out a special edition of the *Herald*, headlined "Crockett Defends the Alamo," with a black-and-white photograph of Tam pushing himself up with a bandaged arm on the chest of the lineman and the other stretching for the ball.

Most of the five hundred or so residents of Dell City turned out the next weekend for a parade down Main Street, and Jack's people barbecued an entire steer for the occasion. There was plenty of beer drinking, and the mayor gave a speech about "enduring small-town values."

But it was all a little anticlimactic for Crockett and Tam, who sensed they had taken the last ride in their high school rodeo. While they would always be Cougars, and nobody could ever take away this magical undefeated season or state championship, they were nearing a fork in the road that would take each of them down a very different path. Their pickups were parked under the water tower behind the Two T's Grocery a block away from the festivities, facing opposite directions so they could lean out the window to talk.

"I'ma spend a few hours with Lola Mae. Then let's meet at the fifteen-seventy-six turnoff. I'll bring the .30, and we'll plink some shit and hang."

"All right."

Lola Mae was a small-town girl, but smart and certainly nobody's fool. She knew that Crockett was probably going to West Point, possibly to war one day, which could mean she might never have that dream of a house with him on the Laws' farm full of little football players and cheerleaders. Growing up amid the harsh give-and-take of farming life in the West Texas desert, Lola Mae had a keen understanding of how the arc of life could bend in heartbreaking directions. Lola Mae wanted to explain that to Crockett today, a few months before their fork in the road, and to give herself fully to him. It was a chilly December day, so she included her old white blanket in the basket of food for a picnic at their favorite spot near an abandoned cotton gin in a remote part of the farm.

They sat close on the blanket, picking at the fried chicken, watching the sun drop behind Otero Mesa, and admiring the pastel shades that one takes for granted living so many years in the high desert. A lock of brown hair had fallen across Lola Mae's face, and she slowly pushed it behind one ear in a distinctly languid, sensuous motion for a seventeen-year-old girl. She gently brushed a crumb from Crockett's chin, pausing for a moment before running her tongue along his lower lip.

"Do you think God is here now, Crockett?"

"I suppose so. The pastor says he's everywhere all the time."

"When I was little, I used to think that he went to sleep when we did, when Mom turned off the lights and closed my door."

The sun was gone now, and Lola Mae lit a candle.

"Let's pretend he's asleep."

Lola Mae lay back on the blanket, and the two young lovers explored their full bodies, their full passions. It was the first time for her, and a few drops of blood fell on the white blanket. "That's our bond, Crockett."

It was almost midnight before Tam and Crockett met at the head of the dirt road just off fifteen seventy-six, too dark to shoot, but they still took turns firing at the stars with Jack's old lever-action 30.30. The Zarkans were not gun people, and most of what Tam had learned about shooting came from Crockett, Jack, or Ray. They both respected guns and gun culture, with a practical understanding of the need for such tools in the lives of farmers living where they did. Crockett slid the rifle into the faded leather scabbard, and the two friends sat in comfortable silence on the tailgate of the pickup.

"So, what's it gonna be?"

"West Point. You?"

"UTEP, preferred walk-on. How'd you leave it with Lola Mae?"

"Good. But who knows? The military, war, and all that shit."

"There's a prayer in the Qur'an for people heading down a new road. I don't remember it all, just this part. 'Guide us to the straight path. The path of those upon whom You have bestowed favor, not of those who have evoked Your anger, or those who are astray.'"

Crockett thought about that for a few moments, then pulled out his old Case toothpick knife.

"There's an Indian tradition about how two people are bonded for life by mixing blood."

"I know it."

Crockett sliced his palm and extended it to Tam, along with the knife. Tam did the same—the blood of the Muslim and the Christian, the Syrian and the American, the two Texans, flowing together under the perfect stars over Dell City.

"Blood brothers."

CHAPTER 12

July 1, 1985, was R-Day—reception day—at West Point, the day Crockett and almost a thousand of his fellow plebes reported for their first of four years in the Long Gray Line that stretched back 183 years. Ray, Bitsy, and Lola Mae sat in bleachers with other parents as the plebes tried their best to march in perfect military formation across the plain toward the commandant, Brigadier General Peter J. Boylan, who would say a few words before administering the oath to new recruits.

The day had been a whirlwind of emotion and activity for Crockett, starting at ten in the morning when he said goodbye to his family. He had hugged Ray and Bitsy, who was imagining how Douglas MacArthur's mother had felt at that moment in 1899, and Lola Mae, tears pouring down her cheeks. R-Day is a symphony of logistics, intended to keep plebes so busy and confused that they have no room for thoughts of home. But Crockett's thoughts kept floating back to Dell City, and to Tam.

Crockett was ushered to the gym, where there was a barrage of fitness tests and medical exams, and then to the barber, where he was shorn like a sheep on a spring day in Dell City. Crockett was issued all the clothes he'd need for the first year: raincoat, gray shirts, sweat suits, cotton gloves, swimsuits, gym shorts, undershirts, a bathrobe, waist belts, shoulder belts, black socks, white shirts, suspenders, boxer shorts, uniform shoes, rubber overshoes, slippers, sneakers, and an array of caps for every occasion. He received a trunk to store all his military equipment—rifle oil, web belt, poncho, and the like—and was shown his room, where security relied on the vaunted honor system rather than locks and keys. There were hours of practicing the proper way to march, salute, stand, dress, and address superiors—all under constant haranguing from upperclassmen.

Crockett was drenched in sweat and pretty well spent by the time he and the other plebes took the oath from General Boylan, who instructed them to raise their right hands and repeat after him.

"I, Crockett Laws, do solemnly swear that I will support the Constitution of the United States and bear true allegiances to the national government; that I will maintain and defend the sovereignty of the United States, paramount to any and all allegiance, sovereignty, or fealty I owe to any state or country whatsoever."

Crockett fell into bed at ten when he heard taps. *What the fuck*, he thought, *when do we start playing football?*

Tam had just started summer football conditioning at UTEP, and he was feeling a little sore but otherwise content as he stood in line for dinner at the team cafeteria. As always, there was a steady stream of music blaring from a boom box: Duran Duran, Madonna, and Phil Collins for the city boys; Lee Greenwood, Ronnie Milsap, and Ricky Skaggs for the country boys; Doug E Fresh, LL Cool J, and Schoolly D for the homeboys. Tam was usually the largest person in any given room, but looking around at eighty or so teammates shucking and jiving to the music, he began to understand just how small a fish he was in this pond. Hell, some of the running backs were his size, and a few of the linemen had him by a hundred pounds.

The coaches would have made accommodations for Tam's dietary restrictions if he had been a scholarship player, but as a walk-on, he was on his own in the chow line to figure out what meat was halal, prescribed under Muslim rules. No big deal, really, since it had been that way at every table in Dell City, except for the ones at his mother's or grandmother's house. But he felt a twinge of nostalgia, of loneliness, thinking about Bernia's chile rellenos, Syrian style.

Tam had driven himself into El Paso for the move to college, two boxes, a suitcase, a duffel bag, and a backpack in the bed of the pickup. A tear-filled family farewell seemed silly since Dell City was only ninety miles away, and Tam could see them pretty much whenever he wanted. The Zarkans had a big dinner together the night before Tam left, and Orhan gave him the Islamic crescent necklace that Ali had worn through-out World War II.

He dropped everything off at the football dorm, where he had a single room, a benefit of being an athlete at UTEP, and walked to the Durham Sports Center for orientation, a physical, and conditioning. The players broke into position groups to establish baselines for strength and speed. Among the nine linebackers, Tam benched 270, which put him in the bottom third, and ran a 4.7 second 40-yard dash, slower only than the future NFL star Seth Joyner. The coach handed out thick notebooks full of defensive schemes, plays, and assign-ments, pulling Tam aside as the meeting broke.

"There's two things we can't measure out there, Tam: heart and brains. I was at the state championship, and I have no doubt about the former. And you should know, you had the highest SATs of all the linebackers, by two hundred points. You're gonna be fine."

Tam was an only child, but he felt part of a bigger family with the Laws, and Crockett was every bit the brother he never had. Driving out of Dell City a few days earlier, he'd stopped for some fried chicken at the Two T's Grocery, and Eula had been there buying a pack of Camels. "Get a dog, Tam. You'll always have a friend, and it will keep you out of trouble." Just before he fell asleep that first night at UTEP, Tam decided that was exactly what he would do.

CHAPTER 13

West Point requires plebes to write an occasional letter home—most of them a few sentences scrawled during those three hours a day that they are not in class, studying, training, eating, or, in Crockett's case, practicing football—and they must show it to their squad leader. Crockett had complied throughout the year, but after stoically enduring ten months of purgatory, he felt like opening the floodgates to someone.

April 7, 1985

Dear Abuela Marcie,

It's Easter today, a beautiful spring morning way up here in the Hudson Valley, and we were allowed to sleep in a bit and take the morning off. I'm reminded of other Easters back home when you would try to hide those colored eggs behind a cactus or under a rock. I'd toddle around wearing that dopey Eton Suit from Mom—the British one with that ridiculous hat—while Abuelo and Dad trailed close behind with .22 pistols, rat shot loaded in case one of those egg-sucking sidewinders found one before me.
I miss all that, and you.

It was fun seeing you all at Christmas, but I never really had the chance to get all this off my chest without sounding like a whiner. I want to tell someone what it's really like, without all the rah-rah bull, and I know you'll understand. You raised me to be a leader, a thinker, and not "the sheep at the back of the flock trotting to the butcher." Hah! Remember that one, Abuela?

It's been tough this first year, starting with what they call "Beast Barracks," those five weeks before school actually starts and all us plebes are allowed to say only twelve words to upper-class cadets: "yes, sir"; "no, sir"; "sir, I do not understand"; and "no excuse, sir." We march and march and march, and they are always waking us up in the middle of the night to line up, salute, do push-ups, change clothes in five minutes, and do it again. The grub is pretty good, but us plebes have to serve meals from trays and know every detail about everyone at our table, like who wants Tabasco or seasoned salt. Imagine, all four thousand cadets eat three meals together in forty minutes! I live in the MacArthur Barracks (Mom loves that!) and share my room with a black guy from Alabama, who's decent but snores like Dad.

There's barely time to play football, and it seems beside the point. I'm not the stud here that I was back in six-man, and they switched me to safety. I didn't play much, mostly special teams, but I returned a kickoff at the Peach Bowl, which we won 31-29. I only made it about twenty yards, but at least I didn't fumble. And at the Navy game, which we lost 17-7, some army paratroopers jumped right onto the 50-yard line. I'm coming to realize there are more important things than football.

There's women here too, more than 10 percent, and Lord knows how or why they're doing it, although I have to say some of them are tough as a boot. It's funny to think

*about Lola Mae doing this, but I'll bet Aunt Eula would
be just fine. The women don't usually run as fast or do
as many pull-ups, but they can tear it up in this crazy
swimming test that's supposed to simulate a confusing
combat situation. We jump from the high board in full
gear, all kinds of flashing lights and loud noises going off,
and have to swim through an underwater obstacle course.
We have to box, which Tam would like, and we also fight
with these padded clubs—Tam would really like that. I
miss that guy, Lola Mae too . . . all of you.*

*And everybody is smart, real smart; sometimes it
seems like I'm the dumbest one here. They barely taught
algebra at our high school, and most of our classes are
related to engineering. Don't worry; I'm a quick study
and, at this point, in the top 25 percent of my class! The
classrooms are spic and span, with all the latest technology, like computers. And we have to leave it spic and span
afterward, not one little mark on the chalkboard. Lucky
for me we do everything in teams, which kinda makes
sense since one of the main points here is preparing us to
lead groups in war.*

*I know you don't like to hear that, Abuela, but that's
probably where I'm heading in four years, especially with
all that turmoil in the Middle East. We also study some
about international relations, and I'm starting to understand how it all fits together: the different kinds of Arabs,
the Soviet Union, the oil, the Jews. Seems to me that oil
plays a big part in all of this. They ought to just forget
about all that Arab oil and use what we've got in Texas.
I've been doing a lot of thinking about war and being
patriotic. They try to brainwash us in all that, what with
medals, inspiring stories, speeches from famous people
like President Reagan, the graveyard full of all those war
heroes. They try to hold us to a higher standard and expect*

us to live by an honor code: "A cadet does not lie, cheat, or steal, or tolerate those who do. Quibbling, cheating, evasive statements, or recourse to technicalities will not be tolerated." Nice words, but they don't hold water when you have our president and his people doing stuff like Iran-Contra. They have something here called "blood branching," that's supposedly been banned, where two guys punch each other in the chest on top of their unit pin and blood spurts everywhere. Some kind of bonding ritual. Like blood brothers, but with all the blood and none of the brotherhood.

You told me all about the Vietnam War—the real story—and I wonder whether they are trying to make us forget about that: the My Lai massacre, the Tet Offensive, the fact that we lost, and all the revolution in the United States about it. There's the most beautiful stained-glass windows in the chapel, and I noticed an inscription on one of them that says, "Quis ut Deus?" I looked it up. Turns out it's a quote from Revelation that means "who is like God?" Who is like God, Abuela? Who is allowed to take a life, and why? Does killing for our country make us gods? I wonder how I'll feel if I ever kill someone. Sorry to weigh you down with these heavy thoughts, but I think them and need to talk to someone about it.

Unfortunately, we won't have a chance to talk this summer because I'll be spending most of it at Camp Buckner, our military training site. Please tell everyone hello, particularly Lola Mae. We had a great time together when she came up a few months ago, and we spent the weekend in New York City. We saw that play Big River, about the adventures of Huckleberry Finn, and stayed at the Plaza Hotel.

All My Love, Crockett.

Marcie folded the letter and slid it back into the fancy West Point–branded envelope. Looking into the valley from the porch on the hill, she felt like crying, although she wasn't quite sure whether her tears would be from sadness or joy. It's like that with kids and grandkids: the internal conflict between pride and sorrow one feels with a first step, a graduation, a marriage. Marcie wrote a reply before her intense emotions subsided.

April 10, 1985

Dear Crockett,

There is only one God, but he has many names—Tam calls him Allah. None of us should ever confuse ourselves with God just because we can kill. There are many references to a "just war" in the scriptures, like this passage in the New Testament, Romans 13:4: "For he is God's servant for your good. But if you do wrong, be afraid for he does not bear the sword in vain. For he is the servant of God, an avenger who carries out God's wrath on the wrongdoer."

A time may come when you will kill. Do so only with the greatest of remorse, and only if you are sure it is for a just cause. You will know the difference, Crockett. And when it comes time to pull the trigger, make sure you shoot straight so that it's the other guy going to heaven, not you!

All the love in my heart, Abuela Marcie

CHAPTER 14

The life of a D1 walk-on, even a preferred walk-on like Tam, pretty much sucks. You spend most of the time on the scout team as cannon fodder for the starters, or standing on the sidelines adjusting your jock and hovering near your position coach hoping he remembers your name. A week into summer practice, the defensive coach gave Tam a chance after the second-team middle linebacker twisted his ankle against the first-team offense.

Tam had paid attention during film study and recognized a fullback counter when quarterback Sammy Garza took the snap, stepped to his right, and then lowered the ball to his left hip. Tam shot the gap between the guard and tackle just as Garza handed the ball to fullback Vic Stagliano, a five-foot-eleven, 208-pound fireplug. Tam had been waiting for this moment, craved the lightning-like transfer of energy he hadn't felt since his days in six-man. Stagliano was explosive and ran close to the ground, too close for Tam. All he remembered about that moment was a white flash exploding in his head, the trainer standing over him afterward asking how many fingers he was holding up, and the coach telling him to "rub some dirt on it." Tam's first concussion, one that would have him retching all night at the dorm and dreaming about massive linemen crushing his wrist. But a D1 walk-on doesn't earn a scholarship in rehab, so Tam stayed on the field for another series, not a single moment of which he could remember.

Tam saw some playing time that first year, the entire second half in a 55-19 loss to Utah, mostly due to UTEP's dismal 1-10 season, which would prove to be the head coach's last. Tam was awarded Scout Team Player of the Year at the football banquet, which gave him a small place in the Miners' trophy case at the Durham Sports Center and a partial scholarship that covered half his tuition the following year. Tam had a half-dozen minor concussions that season, dismissed by the defensive coach as having his "bell rung," and the headaches didn't stop until Christmas break.

But there was a hole in Tam's life that first semester at UTEP, a spot that had been filled the first eighteen years of his life in Dell City with Crockett and his family. He remembered Eula's words about a dog and drove up North Mesa to the Crossroads Animal Hospital the same day the vet called to tell him that there was a new litter of puppies. Tam had told the vet a few months ago he was looking for a puppy—nothing fancy, not too big, loyal, tough, patient, good with kids, likes water.

The vet led Tam to a room off the surgery area, where a pile of puppies slept. They were a jumble of chubby black-and-white-flecked pups tucked close to their mom's warm tummy, nose to tail in a way that made it impossible to tell where one started and the other one ended. A couple of them were dreaming in the way that puppies do, flopping their legs as if they were running after something and whimpering softly. The vet explained that the seven puppies were the offspring of a yellow lab and an Australian cattle dog, a blue heeler. One of the pups popped her head up, yawned a big sleep puppy yawn, and rested her chin on the edge of the little wooden enclosure. She wagged the very tip of a tail, which was nearly as long as her body, and just before she fell asleep, Tam noticed the blue eyes. Tam bent down to rub her head and got a whiff of sweet puppy breath.

"One of these will fit the bill for what you want, Tam. Friendly, smart, loyal, love the water—perfect for a farm in Dell City and a real chick magnet at college."

Someone had walked into the room and stood unnoticed behind them. "Chick magnet, Tam?"

Tam turned around. "Almira!"

"You two know each other."

"Not really. Met once last year after a football visit. What are you doing here?"

"I volunteer every now and then through the animal shelter. Get the occasional dog fix. She's a cute one. I call her Blue."

"Blue?"

The melancholy Tam had been feeling for months suddenly lifted, optimism rushing in where just a few hours before there had been nothing but a big empty hole. Tam left the clinic with Blue and with Almira's telephone number, just in case, she said, he needed a dog sitter.

The granularity of Tam's life began to come into focus after that. Blue was his constant companion, even though house training took a few weeks, and her gentle breathing on the bed at night helped him sleep. Blue couldn't lie close enough to Tam, and on cold nights he'd take her under the covers. Blue was a link between Tam and Almira that gave them a legitimate excuse to see each other several times a week, and she looked after the puppy when Tam had football or class. Blue was on her back exhausted one late afternoon, all four feet in the air, tongue out sideways while Tam and Almira scratched her tummy after an hour of tossing a tennis ball on the practice field next to Sun Bowl Drive. Nobody was more surprised than Tam when Almira leaned over and kissed him.

Tam had found the solid footing that would sustain the rest of his freshman year and take him through college, but there was still unrest about what would happen after that. What would be his purpose in life? Tam still prayed, although not always five times a day, and he sometimes wondered what Allah had planned for him. He could see a path back to Dell City and life on the farm raising kids with Almira, if she would have him. But was that it? Tam imagined how life would be after West Point for Crockett, serving the nation as Ali had done in World War II. On a whim, Tam had stopped by the campus ROTC office, and the captain pitched him hard when he found out Tam spoke Arabic, but he would never have time for it with football and studies. Something to discuss with his family and Crockett back home during Christmas break.

CHAPTER 15

The rape in Juarez had stolen something from Eula, something no amount of warmth or nurturing from Marcie, Sana, and Bernia could restore. They didn't know, couldn't know, how it felt to be stripped and held down in a rancid puddle of muddy water behind the Kentucky Club, brutalized in the most demeaning, nonchalant way. She had nightmares about it, about the callused hands, the weight of them on her body, their words, and the grunting of the young one the moment he entered her. Most of all the shame she felt when Orhan found her, and that look on his face. It was cold comfort that Jack and Ali had killed them.

But Eula was tough and resilient. And in place of what they had taken, Eula now had something hard and jagged, something that gave her a cold determination to survive, to prevail.

Her music was a place to retreat, a place those three dead rapists had not touched, and in some ways a small patch of innocence survived there. Eula was an accomplished strummer, as facile with a flamenco guitar as a pedal steel, but she was drawn to the tawdry simplicity of country music. Eula's voice teacher at the University of Texas was convinced she had the pipes to make it in opera, but the smoking and the whiskey had left her with a rasp better suited for those sad ballads about old cowboys, pickup trucks, and broken hearts. She became something of a local sensation and cultivated her image as the sassy, bad-ass blonde whose music was as good as the one-liners she hurled at the occasional unruly drunk. By the time graduation rolled around in the late 1960s, Eula had made a name for herself opening for the likes of B.B. King, Willie Nelson, and Ray Wiley Hubbard at such legendary venues as The Scoot Inn, The Victory Grill, and the Broken Spoke. Ray and Bitsy, an officer at the Tri Delt sorority, were already well on the road to marriage, and it grounded Eula somewhat to throw back a few mezcals with them and reminisce about the good old days in Dell City. Despite Bitsy's persistent attempts to woo Eula into Greek life, she recoiled at the drunken advances of college boys in their starched jeans and Polo shirts. One late night at the ATO house after a UT football game, Eula decked a kid from Houston who had grabbed her ass on the dance floor. Eula seemed to gravitate toward the poetic castaways who hovered on the fringes of the country music scene—roadies, bartenders, drummers, and the like—and went home with her share for a one-off night of casual sex. The other eye on her budding music career, Eula also took into her bedroom a few of the club owners and bookers who held so much power in that industry.

Jack Kerouac's *On the Road* was like a bible to her, Dean Moriarty her perfect man, and she had read James Michener's *The Drifters* in four days when it came out a year or so after graduation. Like so many young people of that era, she was drawn to the East, and the Beatles *Magical Mystery Tour* had a profound impact on her music. She dropped the bombshell one night playing guitar around the firepit outside Jack and Marcie's house on the farm in Dell City. Eula had spent a few years after graduation playing gigs around Texas, which Jack noted was not "particularly sustainable."

"You have that business minor, and I could use someone to help me with that end of things on the farm."

Marcie shifted uncomfortably in her chair, having cautioned Jack earlier to "put a little honey on it" with Eula when he raised the issue with her. "What Dad means to say, Eula, is what's your fallback?"

"I don't have a fallback, Mom. I have a career. I've saved up some money, and I'm going to India. There's a place to study classical guitar in Varanasi—that old city where people spread their ashes in the Ganges River—and to study meditation in the north, in Rishikesh, with the same guy as the Beatles did. My therapist thinks it's a good idea."

It was as if Jack had been popped in the crotch with a high-voltage cattle prod. "And smoke dope!"

Eula stopped him dead in his tracks. "Daddy, I haven't had a day of peace since Juarez. I can't find it in Austin, and I can't find it in Dell City."

Marcie knew Eula and knew the conversation was over before it started. "Just promise you'll come back to us."

"Promise."

Three months later, after a few weeks hanging out with the Euro expat crowd amid the huts and beaches on the island of Ko Samui off the east coast of Thailand, she stepped from the plane at Kolkata Airport outside Calcutta. A tanned blond woman with a guitar and a backpack, clearly on the Hippie Trail from Southeast Asia, was an easy mark for the taxi drivers lined up at the airport in the early hours of another hot, muggy day. But they hadn't bargained for a West Texas gal like Eula. Without hesitating, she stuffed a few rupees into the hand of the first driver in line and gave him the address of the Evergreen Guest House that a Swedish boy in Ko Samui had written out in Hindi on a piece of paper. "*Jaldee jaldee.*" Quick, quick.

Eula knew that cows were sacred in the Hindu parts of India, but she wasn't quite prepared to see so many of them with garlands, bells, and multicolored designs wandering around the streets on the predawn drive into Calcutta. Her main interaction with cattle had come during branding season on the farm, or with a rack of their smoked ribs on a plate at Marcie's table. It tickled her in a way that brought back some of that innocence of her early youth, sitting on a fencepost watching some cowboy on a quarter horse working a herd. The bundles of rags on almost every corner puzzled her, until a homeless woman and a crippled child emerged from one of them at a stoplight to hold out their helpless, emaciated arms in hopes of a few rupees. The road from the airport was a strategic begging spot, with all the new Western tourists driving by, and Eula didn't disappoint.

Eula spent a few days in Calcutta, sipping espresso, eating samosas, smoking Ganesh beedies and discussing politics, literature, or music with other searchers who had made it to India on a shoestring. Most of them had smoked so much dope by midafternoon that Eula could hardly follow their conversations under the ceiling fans at Café 48, not too far from the Royal Calcutta Lawn Bowling Club. But they would vibrate with delight, particularly the Germans, when she pulled out her guitar in Sudhanand Park and play a lonesome country song under a Banyan tree. She became something of a legend in just a few days, and those whose minds were so clouded with Nepalese hash oil that they couldn't remember her name simply referred to Eula as "that American cowgirl."

Eula's new friends, a rollicking, dancing crowd of about a dozen Western gypsies in baggy cotton Aladdin pants, colorful vests, and voluminous paisley flying skirts, gave her a big sendoff at Chitpur Station, where she would catch the train for an overnight journey to Varanasi. Eula booked an air-conditioned two-tier sleeper, an AC2, and hoisted her gear on the top bunk near two families, as far away as possible from a group of Indian soldiers passing around a bottle of Bagpiper whiskey. Eula tried to breathe through a wave of anxiety, as her therapist had taught her, at the thought of what liberties a bunch of drunken Indian soldiers might think they could take in the middle of the night with an attractive American woman traveling alone. And one of them did make a pass at her, only to receive a sharp whack on his hand with the steel end of a rattan walking stick from a fleshy grandmother in the lower bunk.

The real India began to unpeel for Eula with every mile the train traveled from Calcutta. The rainy season of late summer had ended, the savannahs were a sea of green teeming with wildlife, and just before nightfall the train had to slow down for an elephant cow to gently nudge its calf across the tracks. Through the night, Eula knew the train was pulling into a station when she would hear calls of "Chai!" from a vendor selling the sweet milky tea served in light brown ceramic cups. India was a land of startling contradictions, filth amid serenity, which Eula discovered every time she opened the door to the loo and the rancid smell of questionable hygiene assaulted her. An Australian woman about Eula's age noticed her obvious disgust on one of those visits to relieve herself and offered her a puff from a trumpet-shaped pipe full of hash and tobacco. "Chillum helps." Eula took a long, harsh draw before returning to her bunk and fell asleep within minutes to the rhythmic *click-clack* of the wheels.

As the train passed over the Ganges River, the gateway to Varanasi, the sun was rising, and Eula saw bathers in the water amid an occasional puff of smoke. Eula discovered later that the smoke came from the imploding heads of cremating corpses. Manikar Ghat, one of the few where cremation is permitted, became Eula's favorite spot in Varanasi, showing her a path toward healing and toward understanding the interconnectedness of life and death—the Yin and Yang between body and spirit.

It didn't come easily for Eula, but she began to feel that balance in her life, the balance that had been ripped out in Juarez, returning as the months passed at the Academy of Indian Classical Music. Eula liked her guru, her mentor, and naturally fell into her role of *shishya*, or student. She took naturally to the sitar, although it took some months to adjust from the six strings of her guitar to the twenty-one strings of the oddly shaped, ancient instrument. During private moments in her sparse room, Eula explored ways to work the sitar into some of her country songs, pioneering a sound that would bring her a degree of fame in the cosmic cowboy culture that had begun to emerge in Texas. She lived like a nun during those six months, abstaining from alcohol and men, and felt as close to pure as she had ever been. When it came time to leave, Eula's mentor gave her his personal *mezrab*, a kind of pick used by sitar players. He had sensed the wounds in Eula, and much of what they shared took the form of music. Words seemed inadequate. The guru and *shishya* simply bowed in deep respect to each other, palms pressed together in front of their chests, and Eula melted into a crowded street, backpack slung over one shoulder, guitar over the other.

Eula arrived a few days later in the town of Rishikesh, nestled along the Ganges River at the foot of the Himalayas, where she would study transcendental meditation and practice yoga with Maharishi Mahesh Yogi. The Beatles—accompanied by an entourage of wives, girlfriends, managers, and groupies—had catapulted the Maharishi into international fame when they studied there a few years earlier and introduced transcendental meditation to the West. Their visit, just after release of their wildly popular *Magical Mystery Tour*, would profoundly change their lives and their music, best captured in the song "Across the Universe." Eula would listen to it over and over during her time in India. "*Jai guru deva, om.*"

Eula didn't much care for the hype around that visit, or

the seemingly pious spiritual tourists who had flocked there from the West. She remained aloof from it, nurturing her tranquility with meditation, yoga, and music, which formed a bond between her and the Maharishi. He delighted in Eula's sitar compositions, particularly the adaptations of her country music, and the two unlikely friends—the Hindu mystic and the Texas cowgirl—spent many evenings together during her four months at the ashram. It was during one of those sessions that he introduced Eula to Dexter Winslow, an army veteran from Driggs, Idaho, who had come to the ashram to restore what had been torn from his soul during combat in the Central Highlands of Vietnam. They had a natural affinity, both of them coming from the rural American West. Dexter could sit for hours listening to Eula's music, and laughter came to her naturally when he told stories about his bumbling adjustment from a ranch in Idaho to Princeton, where he had studied philosophy before enlisting in the army.

Dexter had survived the Battle of Dak To, three weeks of intense fighting intended by the North Vietnamese military to distract American and South Vietnamese forces as they prepared for the Tet Offensive. More than a third of the squadron Dexter commanded died in the first week of combat, and the rest of them all received Purple Hearts for wounds sustained during the remainder of the operation. Dexter told Eula all about it one night on a bench near their huts, staring into the distance for three hours as it all came pouring out.

"Killed plenty; stopped counting after that first week. There was this one VC soldier, couldn't have been more than sixteen. Shot him in the stomach. He was dying at our feet, gut shot, screaming like hell, and my sergeant cut off his ears. Just like that. Stuffed those ears in his pocket for Lord knows what."

"And you were wounded?"

"Shot in the shoulder. Didn't seem that bad until I was evacuated, and the doc said it was close to my heart."

"Show me."

Dexter opened his shirt to her, revealing a scar that began as a dark, round mark below his collarbone and ran in a jagged, raised line to his armpit. Eula ran her finger slowly along the scar, up to his cheek, and cupped his chin in her hand. "I'm glad you lived." She took him by the hand into her room. Dexter was the first man Eula had been with in more than a year and, she thought, the first time it had ever felt natural in the way that her God had intended.

Both of them knew it was not a forever thing, but those two months punctuated their lives and gave each of them a new chapter to write. They never saw each other again after their time at the ashram, but there was more than a little surprise on Marcie's and Jack's faces when Eula stepped off the plane in El Paso with a baby girl. India was her name.

Eula was on stage and on fire with the other two members of her band—the Karma Cowgirls—at the Electric Ballroom in Dallas. She was rocking a sitar version of "Lone Star Dharma," a regional hit that KZEW was playing almost every hour, and the crowd was on its feet singing along. The Karma Cowgirls ended the show with Eula's favorite song, "Dexter," a country-ish ballad that Eula sang alone, a cappella. Marcie was standing offstage, watching the show and swaying with her granddaughter in her arms. She came out with the Cowgirls for the encore and handed the one-year-old to Eula. Babe in her arms, guitar at her side, Eula sang a song she had written for her daughter, titled simply "India."

CHAPTER 16

Crockett's and Tam's lives the previous three years had been like the diagram of an oval, starting at the same point, spreading wide apart in the same direction, and then converging back together and touching again.

Despite his difficulties with studies and his private skepticism about the entire West Point culture, Crockett finished in the top 25 percent of his class, rose to the rank of squad leader, and distinguished himself during field exercises. In the hills above West Point at Camp Buckner— where cadets spend seven weeks during the summer before their final year, training in simulated combat under the guidance of officers from the 101st Airborne Division—Crockett was every inch the field general from his Cougar football days in Dell City. The entire seven weeks—which hone a cadet's skills in infantry tactics, artillery fundamentals, armor maneuver, field craft, weapons employment, navigation, and hand-to-hand combat—is an endurance test.

On a hot night five weeks into Camp Buckner, Crockett found himself and half the men under his command separated and pinned down behind a cluster of buildings under simulated enemy fire while on a search-and-rescue mission in what was supposed to be a dense neighborhood in the Arab Middle East.

Communications with the other half of his squad had been cut, and a scout gave him a breathless account that the "terrorists" were preparing to kill the two hostages. *Muslim terrorists, no doubt*, Crockett thought cynically. His men, sweat pouring from under their helmets, gave him the same "what now, captain?" look as his offensive linemen had given him during the final seconds of the state six-man championship, when Crockett had called a naked quarterback boot and scooted thirty yards into the end zone for the winning score. As a diversionary tactic, Crockett ordered the scout to tell his men on the other side of the town to launch a mortar attack about fifty yards in front of the house where the hostages were being held and to advance on the location with machine-gun fire and smoke grenades. Meanwhile, during the confusion, Crockett and his men, faces blackened with greasepaint, snuck up behind the house. It worked like a charm. The five terrorists had their backs turned when Crockett's group leaped through the windows and kicked down the door. It was over in a few seconds: five "dead" terrorists on the ground and two hostages secured. The trainer, a captain from the 101st, gave them a thumbs-up when they regrouped afterward and offered the highest praise a ranger can give. "Snake eaters all of you, hoo-ah!" To which Crockett's entire squad responded in unison, "Hoo-ah!"

Crockett never cracked the starting lineup on the Black Knights, but he saw plenty of playing time as a fifth defensive back in obvious passing situations. He craved the diversion from military drills and studies and enjoyed the camaraderie during four of the best years ever for the Black Knights, in which they defeated Navy three consecutive times to take home the Commander-in-Chief's Trophy. His firstie teammates elected Crockett legacy captain, entitling him to lead the team onto the field for spring practice.

Finishing in the top 25 percent of his class, Crockett had his first choice of assignments, and he selected Combat

Arms as a tank commander, a childhood dream of his and Tam's since they were kids scrambling around the massive chili picker on the farm. After graduation and a long visit to Dell City, when he asked for Lola Mae's hand, Crockett deployed to Army Officer Armor Basic Training and successfully completed Ranger School. It was similar to Camp Buckner, with a high washout rate, mostly for physical or mental failure. During the fifty-eight-day military leadership course, Crockett learned about mountain, jungle, and desert warfare in Georgia, Florida, and Texas. He was among the 40 percent of his class who earned a Ranger Tab by surviving twenty-hour days toting up to ninety pounds and eating no more than two small meals.

In the summer of 1990, Crockett received his first posting as a tank commander at Fort Bliss outside El Paso, and there was a familiar face in his squad, Sergeant First Class Tamerlane Zarkan. The two friends had stayed in close contact during college, overlapping infrequently in Dell City, and Crockett knew all about Tam's football experiences, Almira, and Blue. But he was still surprised when Tam enlisted in the army after graduation.

Tam had majored in Agriculture at UTEP and fought his way into a starting position on the football team. The head coach was replaced after that miserable first season with a single win, and the Miners improved every year. They managed to land a five-star recruit in 1986 with defensive end Tony Tolbert, who went on to win three Super Bowls with the Dallas Cowboys. With Tolbert on the edge and Tam behind him at weak-side linebacker, the Miners' defense led the team to a 10-3 record in 1988, earning a berth in the Independence Bowl against Mississippi State. It was UTEP's first bowl game in twenty-one years, and they were facing Brett Favre, an unheralded sophomore quarterback who would win a Super Bowl for Green Bay and enter the NFL Hall of Fame in 2016.

Mississippi didn't need Favre's magic that day, with corner-back James Henry returning two punts for touchdowns, but he threw a touchdown pass and was efficient in leading the Eagles to a 38-18 victory over the Miners.

Almira was hunkered down in her carrel at the library that spring when she heard the clicking of nails on the wooden floor and felt Blue's cold, wet nose flop into her lap, with an envelope in her mouth that contained a letter with only four words: "*Ahbak*"—"I love you"—in Arabic and "Marry Me, Almira" in English. Tam, whose big head and shoulders popped up from the next carrel, had already secured the permission of Almira's parents. But he didn't want Almira to submit; he wanted her to accept. "*Ahbak*, Tam—yes, of course, yes!" She was less enthusiastic about Tam enlisting in the army, but she knew how much he felt it was a matter of service to his country and supported him as she would for their entire life together in a world that would become more confusing and dangerous every year.

Tam breezed through fifteen weeks of basic and advanced armor training at Fort Knox, Kentucky's US Army Armor School, where he learned every inch of the M1A1 Abrams tank. Tam was a natural for the military, his Arabic language skills coveted in an army focused on the threats emerging from the Middle East, and by the time he was stationed at Fort Bliss, he had risen to the rank of sergeant first class.

There was growing angst in the Middle East over the intentions of Iraqi strongman Saddam Hussein, who seemed to have his eyes on the rich oil fields of Kuwait and Saudi Arabia, and speculation in the ranks at Fort Bliss about how President Bush might respond. When the pace of contingency planning accelerated, Tam and Crockett accelerated their planning for a joint marriage to Almira and Lola Mae in the spring.

CHAPTER 17

Tam and Crockett both wore black cowboy boots at their wedding.

It was Tam's first tuxedo, and Crockett adjusted his friend's tie around the collar of the wingtip shirt. Crockett, in full West Point dress whites, had grown adept due to the countless times he had been forced to change uniforms during midnight hazing sessions his first year at West Point. Crockett looked every inch a hardened warrior who cleaned up well in his white waistcoat with polished gold buttons, crisp black bowtie, black pants, and the epaulets of a second lieutenant. The cowboy boots were the only deviation from the West Point dress code, but Crockett didn't give a damn, even if the academy superintendent were to walk in.

Jack and Ray sipped whiskey in the corner of the room with Lola Mae's father, Wilbur Kincaid, a successful farmer in Dell City. Ali, Orhan, and Almira's father, Farez, all of whom looked as if they could have used a drink, went over their duties during the ceremony and checked the ring pouch hanging from Blue's collar. Marcie, Bernia, Lola Beth, and Lola Mae's mother, Radie, fussed with the two brides' dresses. Eula sat on the couch tuning her guitar and sitar, while India, the five-year-old flower girl, practiced throwing bluebonnets in the air. Bitsy was a whirling dervish, spinning through the hotel bossing the staff around about flower arrangements and place cards. The brides were a stunning contrast in Western and Eastern beauty: Lola Mae in the traditional full-length white dress in which her mother and grandmother had been married, tailored with a lower neckline and see-through lace sleeves, and Almira, a fairy tale Muslim princess in a full-length mermaid chiffon gown with a lace neckline and hijab. Looking at his daughter, Farez felt a tinge of sadness that her mother, who had succumbed to breast cancer two years earlier, could not be there to see it.

Ali, Orhan, and Farez had resisted Jack's offer to foot the bill for the entire three-day affair, knowing full well they would go into hock underwriting a half share for such an extravagant event. They insisted on paying for all the Muslim parts, the costliest being food that complied with Islamic dietary rules. The entire three days would take place at the Gage Hotel in Marathon, 220 miles southeast across the desert from Dell City. The Gage was an iconic cowboy hotel that had been restored with elegance and authenticity, right down to the wooden mail slots behind the front desk and the eight-foot stuffed grizzly pawing the air in the corner of a small banquet room in which one could imagine Sam Houston and Davy Crockett smoking cigars over a game of seven-card stud. The entire place belonged to the Laws and the Zarkans: thirty-five rooms, five freestanding casitas, the large covered patio out back for dancing, the White Buffalo Bar with a real white buffalo head on the wall, and the 12 Gage Restaurant with a large Mexican patio ideal for Eula to serenade the guests.

They came in robes and they came in pinstripe suits. And whether they faced east and prayed to Allah or faced a pulpit worshipping the Lord, they all thanked their God when the two couples stood before them in a single golden shaft of light from a setting sun behind the Mexican tile courtyard at the

Gage. Andrew Solomons didn't come in a robe or a suit, but he wore a symbol of his piety too, a yarmulke with a Star of David and a Texas flag.

Weaving together a dual Muslim and Christian marriage ceremony was a tall order, particularly in the middle of the West Texas desert, but well within the diplomatic skills of Marcie, Sana, and Bernia. Their first decision was to keep Jack, Ali, Orhan, and Bitsy out of it. An Islamic marriage required only an *aqd*, a contract between the couple and their families, but wedding ceremonies were commonplace. It was decided that Imam Ibrahim Jalad from the El Paso Mosque would officiate for the *nikah*, the marriage and the contract, during the ceremony at the Gage, and Reverend Jesse Hood from the First United Methodist Church in Alpine would preside over the Christian part.

Tam and Crockett stood to the right of the two preachers, and they turned to the back of the courtyard with the rest of the crowd as Almira and Lola Mae glided down the aisle, followed by India, whose expression alternated between bliss as she tossed bluebonnet petals in the air and red-faced frustration as Blue snapped at the purple petals the moment they left her hand. India kept yanking on her leash, spinning the ring pouch around so much that Ali kept an eye out lest the rings should go flying, and at one point she seemed on the verge of tears until Eula shot her the look that had frozen many a rowdy cowboy in his tracks.

Imam Jalad went first, then Reverend Hood. A Muslim groom is required to give his bride a gift, a *mahr*—for the purposes of this ceremony, a wedding ring. Blue wagged her tail and licked Tam's face as he bent down for the ring and barked when he slipped it on Almira's finger. The imam nodded to Almira, who recited her vows in Arabic, and Tam responded.

"I have given away myself in *nikah* to you, on the agreed *mahr*."

"I have accepted the *nikah*."

After that simple exchange, Tam kissed Almira on the forehead gently, with respect, and they were married.

Reverend Hood then took over, reciting a traditional ceremony in which Crockett and Lola Mae exchanged vows and held each other in their arms for a lingering kiss.

In an article for the *Herald*, Solomons described the wedding and the party as a "bicultural hoedown."

And boy, was there food, twenty feet of it on tables far enough apart to satisfy any Islamic rules. The Zarkan women had worked for days pulling together their side of it: hummus, couscous, grilled halloumi, falafel, baba ghanoush, shawarma, shish tawook, dolmas, baklava dripping with honey, which India grabbed by the handful and slipped occasionally under the table to Blue. And at Tam's request, chile rellenos, Syrian style. Jack's people, under the direction of Marcie and with a little help on the meat from the chefs at the Reata in Alpine, had rolled out Galveston Bay oysters, skillet cornbread, jalapeno cheese grits, coleslaw, okra, deviled eggs, fried chicken, chicken fried steak, smoked brisket, pulled pork, rib eyes, and German chocolate cake with Blue Bell ice cream.

After dinner, the tables were cleared away for dancing, with a few risers in the front for a band. A single haunting note from a steel string floated over the patio as strands of blue, red, and white lights shone on the patio. A shaft of light hit the dark stage. Eula and the Karma Cowgirls, in wild paisley skirts and cowboy boots, stepped out and broke into a song they had composed for the newlyweds: "Salam Alaikum Y'all," a Jimmy Buffet-ish blend of sitar and country about two lovers who sail from the Suez Canal to Padre Island. The music flowed, and everyone danced with everyone, lubricated by a new lager cooked up for the occasion at the Big Bend Brewery in Alpine, and at one point the entire crowd line-danced to the Cotton-Eyed Joe and then to the Syrian Dabke.

Well after midnight, Eula cleared the floor and called out the two couples for a traditional wedding waltz to Anne Murray's "Could I Have This Dance." The music drifted over the desert night. Marcie rested her head on Jack's shoulder as Sana held Ali's hand—all four of them proud and sad at the same time. Eula sang the final refrain—"Can I have this dance for the rest of my life?"—while the newlyweds walked through the crowd, to their wedding beds, and into their new lives.

CHAPTER 18

US Ambassador April Glaspie, a veteran diplomat who led the mission in Baghdad, walked into her meeting on July 25, 1990, with Iraqi President Saddam Hussein under orders from President Bush and Secretary of State James Baker to clarify what he intended by threatening Kuwait and massing troops along the border.

Glaspie: "Normally that would be none of our business, but when this happens in the context of your threats against Kuwait, then it would be reasonable for us to be concerned. For this reason, I have received an instruction to ask you, in the spirit of friendship—not confrontation—regarding your intentions. Why are your troops massed so very close to Kuwait's borders?"

Saddam: "As you know, for years now I have made every effort to reach a settlement on our dispute with Kuwait. There is to be a meeting in two days; I am prepared to give negotiations this one more brief chance. When we meet and we see there is hope, then nothing will happen. But if we are unable to find a solution, then it will be natural that Iraq will not accept death."

Glaspie: "What solution would be acceptable?"

Saddam: "If we could keep the whole of the Shatt al Arab—our strategic goal in our war with Iran—we will make concessions. But if we are forced to choose between keeping half of the Shatt and the whole of Iraq [in Saddam's view, including Kuwait], then we will give up all of the Shatt to defend our claims on Kuwait to keep the whole of Iraq in the shape we wish it to be. What is the United States' opinion on this?"

Glaspie: "We have no opinion on your Arab–Arab conflicts, such as your dispute with Kuwait. Secretary Baker has directed me to emphasize the instruction, first given to Iraq in the 1960s, that the Kuwait issue is not associated with America."

Saddam smiled, like a fox who has just been given the keys to the henhouse, and eight days later his troops invaded Kuwait.

Returning four days later from the presidential retreat at Camp David, Maryland, President Bush bristled with an anger seldom seen from the veteran politician as he spoke to the White House press corps, drawing the kind of line in the sand that could only be backed up with military force if diplomacy failed. "This will not stand."

Three days later, Bush ordered the first of more than five hundred thousand troops to the region and unleashed Baker on a diplomatic effort that would span thousands of miles over five months, culminating with a single decisive meeting on January 9 at the Intercontinental Hotel in Geneva.

A handful of crack reporters had joined Baker on his diplomatic odyssey, including the Associated Press's Barry Schweid, Reuters's Alan Elsner, United Press International's Jim Anderson, Knight Ridder's Susan Bennett, the *New York Times*' Tom Friedman, the *Wall Street Journal*'s Bob

Greenberger, the *Los Angeles Times'* Norman Kempster, the *Washington Post's* Bill Drozdiak, the *Washington Times'* Warren Strobel, ABC's John McWethy, CNN's Ralph Begleiter, and *Newsweek's* Margaret Warner.

The sun was setting on the golden age of journalism, with the web in its infancy and cell phones the size of bricks. Schweid, who had been spun by the best dating back to National Security Advisor Henry Kissinger's secret trip to China in 1971, still used an Olivetti typewriter to bang out his copy and phone it in to whichever overnight editor or intern happened to be on duty in Washington. A few young, tech-savvy reporters, like Strobel, had Tandys with screens the size of a single paragraph and could connect to the guts of a telephone with alligator clips to transmit their stories from infrastructure-challenged cities like Damascus, Beirut, Jordan, or Cairo. The diplomatic beat was a prized gig for reporters, who flew in the back of the airplane, thick as thieves, and picked up some of their best stuff from "senior officials" when a secretary of state or some deputy would stop by their seats on the way to the lavatory. Schweid, a Runyonesque character with a dry rapier wit, brought liar's poker to the back of the plane, and reporters took great pride playing it in the most inappropriate settings: the Vatican, the Great Hall of the People, or on January 9, 1990, in an auditorium at the Intercontinental Hotel in Geneva waiting for Secretary of State James Baker to brief hundreds of reporters on his decisive meeting with Iraqi foreign minister Tariq Aziz.

Seated next to Friedman, an infrequent player, Schweid used hand signals to convey to McWethy, a row back on the other side of the room, the poker hand he was able to conjure from the serial number on a dollar bill. The betting was ricocheting around the room—McWethy, Warner, Kempster, Elsner, and back to Schweid—when Baker's spokeswoman, Margaret Tutwiler, brushed aside the blue curtain behind the podium at the Intercontinental to signal that her boss was on his way out.

Baker had spent five months shuttling between Washington and every major capital from Moscow to London trying to build a coalition of twenty-eight unlikely allies to enforce compliance with eleven UN resolutions and dissuade Saddam—who had taken hundreds of hostages as human shields around strategic targets and occupied Kuwait's oil fields—from leading Iraq into war. Baker was not bluffing in his game of liar's poker with the Iraqis when he stepped before the microphone.

"Regrettably, ladies and gentlemen, I heard nothing today, in over six hours, heard nothing that suggested to me any Iraqi flexibility whatsoever on complying with United Nations Security Council resolutions."

Alan Elsner bolted out of the auditorium to file a flash to the Reuters wire, relying on the local bureau to take his place and sweep up all the b-roll, while the news magazines probed Baker for color to include in tick-tock stories they would file at the end of the week, and the television reporters competed for the microphone so their networks could air footage with them in it.

The first air strikes on Iraq began eight days later.

CHAPTER 19

As Marcie had warned in her letter to Crockett at West Point five years ago, "A time may come when you will kill," and that time was now.

First Armored Division Commander Major General Ron Griffith had 348 M1A1 Abrams tanks under his command in Iraq. Three tank battalions of the Second Brigade, under Colonel Montgomery Meigs, were poised to strike the Iraqi Republican Guard's second tank brigade, the Medina Luminous Division, outside Basra, a large city in the Shatt al Arab between Iran and Kuwait. An M1A1 was parked in the lead of the three tank brigades, with Tam in the driver's seat gripping the motorcycle-style handlebars and Crockett commanding above him in the turret basket next to the loader and the gunner. Crockett reflected on whether this was a "just war," as Marcie had counseled him in her letter. And Tam recited the Muslim prayer for protection against enemies, wondering whether a twenty-five-year-old Iraqi tank driver on the other side of Medina Ridge was doing the same. "O Allah, we ask You to restrain them by their necks, and we seek refuge in You from their evil."

Up until February, Tam, Crockett, and most of their brigade had sat out the war, practicing pulling on their chem-bio protective suits, eating cold MREs, listening to rock music, and writing letters to Almira and Lola Mae, both of whom were in the final stages of their third trimesters. Allied victory was a foregone conclusion, but US air forces were relentless, like a pack of wolves on a bloodied animal. On a single day, they destroyed nearly two thousand vehicles and incinerated thousands of Iraqi soldiers as they fled Kuwait on Highway 8, the Highway of Death.

Although a number of Islamic nations had joined the allied coalition—Saudi Arabia, Syria, Morocco, Kuwait, Oman, Pakistan, the UAE, Qatar, and Bahrain—Tam was troubled at the prospect of killing Muslims and relieved that none had died so far at the business end of his tank cannon. He prayed regularly and openly, and despite warnings from commanders that Muslim American soldiers should not be harassed, nerves frayed during the long boring days, and there had been some tense moments.

There was always towel-snapping, locker-room banter, particularly from the redneck boys who never stopped boasting about their high school football teams or how many cheerleaders they had fucked. And there were not infrequent references to niggers, kikes, or spics, which, needless to say, did not go over well with the blacks, Jews, or Hispanics. Growing up in West Texas, Tam had heard it all and then some. But Crockett had to restrain Tam when Private Otis Baggerley from Irwinville, Georgia, where the US Cavalry captured Confederate States President Jefferson Davis in 1865, ridiculed him for the way he prayed and insinuated that he could be a traitor. "I sure as shit wouldn't want to be sharing a tank with a sand nigger when the shooting starts." A few hours later, during the largest tank battle since World War II, the private would learn just how wrong he was.

Their platoon had been the vanguard in a running battle with Iraqi Republican Guard armor and infantry as they made a desperate dash to the border, where, under UN resolutions, allied forces were supposed to stop. It was a turkey shoot. AH-64 Apache attack helicopters, bristling with Hellfire antitank missiles, and A-10 Thunderbolt IIs, with Avenger Gatling-style guns firing eight-inch chunks of depleted uranium at a rate of four thousand rounds per minute, eviscerated what was left of Saddam's vaunted Republican Guard. Iraqi troops swarmed out of bunkers like ants from a burning nest and surrendered by the thousands, almost eight hundred in the two days leading to the Battle of Medina Ridge. Crockett worked hard to tamp down the dangerous bloodlust in his men that was growing with every kill, and Tam had to remind himself of the murders, rapes, and looting many of those same Republican Guard units had committed during their occupation of Kuwait. Both of them were speechless when their column passed a smoldering Iraqi tank and one of their men joked on the radio about the charred remains of a soldier who must have been consumed in flames and insane with pain as he tried in vain to flee.

"Just how I like my sand nigger: well done."

Crockett yelled into the mike, "Shut the fuck up!"

Dense smoke from Kuwaiti oil wells, which Iraqi forces set ablaze before their retreat, hung over the desert as the American armored column neared Medina Ridge. What remained of Saddam's Adnan division was making a stand, and they had dug in on the other side in a defensive tactic that offered some protection from US missiles and made it impossible to see them until the American tanks crested the hill.

Crockett's tank was the first one over Medina Ridge and narrowly missed being hit by a 125 mm shell fired from a Soviet-made Iraqi T-72 tank not more than fifty yards away. Private Baggerley, who was standing brazenly in the hatch waving his arms and doing some kind of goofy rebel yell, was not so lucky. The Iraqi shell took Baggerley's right arm off a few inches below the shoulder and threw him from the tank. The private tumbled across the desert like a dry leaf in a fall wind and barely missed being crushed by an advancing American tank. Numb and in shock, Baggerley sat up and squeezed his mangled stump, trying to stop the arterial blood spewing from what had been, just a few seconds ago, a living, working arm with a Guns N' Roses tattoo across the triceps. Before Crockett could stop him, Tam leaped from his tank and ran twenty-five yards through the sand to the wounded soldier, tore off his belt, and tightened it around the stump until the bleeding slowed to a sickening drip. Baggerley began slipping into unconsciousness as two medics approached and stabbed a morphine pen into his thigh.

"Zarkan, you taking your pants off?" one of the medics asked.

"Thought I might take a shit as long as I'm out here."

The Islamic crescent necklace had fallen from his neck and into the private's lap.

"Keep it," Tam said, unsure whether his words registered with Baggerley. "Give it back to me later."

It was over in less than five minutes, and Tam was back in the driver's seat of Crockett's M1A1.

"Tam, you son of a bitch. What the fuck would I have told Almira and that kid you'd never meet?"

"You're the West Point man, LT. You'd have figured something out. And you'd teach my son how to run a twenty-three slam."

The Iraqis fought bravely, but the Battle of Medina Ridge was over in less than an hour, with only four American tanks destroyed. The carnage on Iraqi forces was like nothing the American soldiers had ever seen: 186 tanks and 127 armored vehicles destroyed, and not enough left of Iraqi soldiers in the smoking husks of their equipment for the Americans to count the bodies. Sgt. First Class Larry Porter from Portsmouth,

Ohio, recalled the horror of his first time in combat to the *New York Times'* Michael Gordon:

"We have all had a chance to call our wives, and most of the guys couldn't talk about it to them. I don't think my wife needs to know what took place out here. I don't want her to know that side of me."

But there was a glimmer of humanity out there that day in the killing field when a Muslim American soldier fighting an army of Muslims saved the life of a bigoted redneck from Georgia.

CHAPTER 20

At about the same time Tam was saving Baggerley's life, Almira's water broke, and an hour later Lola Mae's.

They had grown close during their husbands' deployment and, like stoic soldiers' wives, had reconciled that their husbands would not be home for the birth. They were both sturdy West Texas working women who had not slowed down much during the first eight months. But moving around was a chore in the final month, leaving Almira and Lola Mae to spend most of their time in Marcie's kitchen with Sana and Bernia. Eula would play some guitar or sitar; India would serenade them while massaging their feet; and Blue, her head resting on Almira's lap, would tilt her head to the side every time the baby moved. Almira's water broke on one of those afternoons, puzzling India, who asked if she'd had "an accident." Everyone, except Blue, had a task assigned for this exact moment, and the women were like a well-drilled military unit as they calmly carried them out. That's when Lola Mae had her "accident," hoisting Almira's suitcase into the bed of Ali's truck.

Ali drove while Sana and Bernia tended to Almira. Jack, Marcie, and Eula did the same in the other truck, while Bitsy, Ray, and Blue stayed behind to take care of the farm and keep an eye on India. It was not much more than an hour's drive into El Paso, but Jack and Ali fretted about making their way through rush-hour traffic to Providence Hospital downtown. As a contingency, they opted for Montana Avenue all the way in rather than risk being snagged in a traffic jam on I-10, but the stoplights were not cooperating. Jack was cursing like a sailor, and Ali must have muttered "*Ya Ibn el Sharmouta*," son of a bitch, a dozen times before they hit the outskirts of El Paso.

The men stayed in the waiting room, thumbing old copies of *Southern Living* and *Texas Monthly*, as the five women—five births among them—accompanied Almira and Lola Mae into delivery. Lola Mae's mother and father—Radie and Wilbur— joined them in the waiting room an hour later. As the families had requested, they would go through labor and delivery together in a suite with a curtain between them. Ali stopped Sana just as the nurses were wheeling Almira into delivery and, in the sheepish manner of an older Muslim man not accustomed to such private female rituals, handed her a small box of dates, which are said to enrich a new mother's breast milk.

Lola Mae's baby crowned around midnight, and with Marcie and Eula holding her legs, she delivered a seven-pound boy within a dozen or so contractions. Almira smiled through her own private pain and in Arabic repeated the Muslim prayer for childbirth.

"O Allah, do not leave me alone, though You are the best of inheritors. Sorrowfulness due to loneliness and sense of abandonment made me fall short of what I should have done to thank You, but give me an upright and honest posterity, male and female. On account of them change my loneliness with companionship and let there be ease and comfort instead of desolation, so that I should thank You on the completion of bounty. O the great giver of greatness, then keep me continuously in ease and comfort, till I am favored with Your pleasure, because of my truthfulness in whatever I say, I promise and I do."

No surprise, given Tam's size, that Almira's birth did not go quite as smoothly, and it took several hours of hard work to push out her nine-pound boy.

Both of them were normal and healthy, curled into little wrinkled balls on their mothers' breasts, although Almira had to laugh when Bernia joked about the size of her son's hands.

Orhan nudged Ali and Jack, who had fallen asleep, when Marcie and Sana poked their heads out of delivery, motioning them all to come in. "All good. Two perfect boys." They eased into the room, Jack with his soiled Marfa Low Crown in his hand; Ali and Orhan the same with their Stetson Lobos. The nurse had slid blue index-size cards with the boys' names into the holder at the foot of the beds: Tamerlane II and Crockett Jr., and in quotation marks, T2 and Deuce.

Jack pulled a small glass vial out of his jeans' pocket and poured a few drops into a thimble. Jack hadn't discussed it with Marcie when he'd done it for Ray and Eula, and he didn't discuss it this time either. "With your permission, Lola Mae. It's a tradition." Then Jack, struggling a little without a thumb on his seventy-nine-year-old right hand, placed a few drops of water from the Bone Springs–Victorio Peak Aquifer on Deuce's lips. Jack and Marcie were the only ones in the room who had any clue that water could one day be worth its weight in gold.

CHAPTER 21

Tam got up in the middle of the night to check on T2, a bruiser at sixteen months, and the new twins: Anil, a small boy with an insatiable need for Almira's milk, and Ademar, a green-eyed girl who never seemed to cry.

He and Crockett had returned to the United States as heroes after the war, with a year of free lunches at Rosita's and eighteen more months stationed at Fort Bliss outside El Paso before satisfying their service obligation. It couldn't come soon enough for Tam and Crockett, who just wanted to hang up their uniforms and put distance between them and the obscenity of war that frequently revisited them in their nightmares. The country was in full swagger after the lopsided victory, the mistake of Vietnam all but forgotten—except for the families of 58,220 dead Americans whose names lined the stark black memorial in Washington, and nearly 1.5 million Vietnamese. Crockett and Tam visited the Vietnam Memorial when they joined eight thousand other service members who paraded down Pennsylvania Avenue for the National Victory Celebration. Tam's mind kept wandering back to Medina Ridge, to Baggerley's arm and all those dead Iraqis, and he knew Crockett was thinking the same thing when President Bush spoke about "the American way."

Tam spent many sleepless nights in the house he had built near his parents on the Laws's farm, and he knew from the lights in the living room at Crockett's that his friend wasn't doing much better. He was careful not to wake Almira or the sleeping kids, particularly Anil, who would take hours to calm down, as he checked some mail. One letter stood out, with a return address in Irwinville, Georgia. When Tam opened it, his Islamic crescent necklace fell out.

Dear Sarge,

When I woke up at the army hospital in Germany, this was around my neck, and I remembered you gave it to me after my arm was blown off at Medina. The nurse asked me if I was Muslim because of it, and I had to laugh. Not out of disrespect, but because of that time I called you a sand nigger.

Pretty stupid calling you that name, and standing up out of the tank. I'll be paying for that one the rest of my days. Life ain't easy without a right arm, but I've gotten pretty good with Ping-Pong and writing with my left hand. My fiancée blew me off, said I was a turnoff in the sack, and it's hard to get through a day without some kind of pain meds or booze. Smoking weed calms me down, helps me see stuff I didn't see before.

One thing I've been doing that I didn't do before is read a lot of books. I read one called The Girl in the Tangerine Scarf, *about a Syrian Muslim girl growing up in the 1970s in Indiana, and it got me to thinking about you. You're Syrian, right? Well, American like me but with kin from Syria. That's kind of the point, I guess. When you jumped out of the tank and saved my life, you didn't care what I was or that I had insulted your religion. You were just helping another American soldier.*

I'm not bitter about my injury. Our God, the God we share, gave me a lesson that day. And I won't forget it, or you. The way I look at it, you were the hand of God that day, and I thank you for it. Who knows what the world will bring, but I have a feeling that there's some shit down the road with all the Muslims if we keep disrespecting them the way I disrespected you.

I wish only good things for you in this life, Sarge. And you'll always have a friend in Irwinville.

As-Salaam-Alaikum,
Otis Baggerley

PART

TWO

CHAPTER 1

Bitsy Laws was on the 104th floor of One World Trade Center in lower Manhattan on Tuesday morning, September 11, 2001. She was on one of her "shopping trips" to New York, code for a weekend of wining, dining, and sex with Jerry Lyons, a vice president at Cantor Fitzgerald whom she'd met several years earlier during Crockett's time at West Point. Ray didn't have a clue, but Eula had sniffed it out from the start when she'd noticed a Victoria's Secret bag in the bottom of Bitsy's closet and called her out. "Do a girl a solid, Eula," Bitsy pleaded, and her sister-in-law kept the secret, forever.

Bitsy was smudging the lipstick from Lyons's cheek at 8:36:40 that morning in his corner office, and the two of them turned to the window just in time to see American Airlines Flight 11 slam into the building five floors below. A massive explosion a few moments later threw them to the floor, violently face-first into Lyons's $27,000 Persian Isfahan silk carpet, breaking Bitsy's nose and her lover's neck. Blood and tears dripped from her chin on Lyons's starched white collar as she tried to revive him, but it was clear to her from the angle of his head that he was dead. With the fire alarm screaming and the sprinklers spewing water, Bitsy crawled to the elevator, but it was frozen in the lobby, and the door on the emergency exit was too hot to touch. Barely able to breathe, she crawled back to the office in hopes there would be fresh air coming in from the broken windows. When she leaned out to suck in fresh air, a black man who had jumped from a few floors up fell past her, headfirst, then another and another, like human snowflakes falling to the street. Bitsy knew it was the end for her; better to jump and get it over with than to burn. She threw one leg over the window sill, then the other, and stood facing out on the narrow ledge, holding the sill behind her with both hands, like a swimmer poised for the starter's pistol. Given the circumstances that had brought her to this moment, Bitsy was ashamed to pray, but she hoped this final desperate act might somehow cleanse her in the eyes of her God. Bitsy imagined how she would look on the pavement 105 stories below and held her skirt tightly at the knees all the way down.

Two thousand miles away in Dell City, Andrew Solomons was at the *Hudspeth County Herald* newsroom watching CNN and waiting for President Bush, W, to address the nation in the wake of what would come to be known simply as 9/11. Al-Qa'ida, the Base, a violent fundamentalist Sunni Muslim group led by Osama bin Laden, had struck a blow to the heartland that would leave no community untouched. Nineteen men—fifteen of them Saudis and all of them from middle-class families—had hijacked four commercial airliners and flown them on suicide missions that yielded a terrorist bonanza: 2,996 people killed, 6,000 injured, and more than ten billion dollars in damage. The greater destruction was to the fabric of American life, ripped so violently on that glorious Indian summer morning that it would never be whole again, at least not in the way it had been in the six decades of relative innocence since World War II.

Well into his seventies, Solomons still ran the *Hudspeth County Herald*, and his priority the morning of 9/11 had been polishing a story on a brewing legal tussle over West Texas water rights, and editing the latest column for "Burr under My Saddle." But like editors from New York to Los Angeles and London to Beijing, Solomons had taken a deep pause to consider how to cover a story that would seep for decades into almost every corner of life. Journalistic muscle memory began to flex itself, as it did with every veteran newsperson that day, and he headed to Dell City High School to scope out a local angle.

The Cougars would play Fort Hancock that Saturday, and the first thing he saw was a banner hanging on the outside wall: "Lasso the Mustangs." The second thing he saw was Tamerlane Zarkan and Crockett Laws clomping down the hallway in muddy goat ropers with four kids in tow: T2, Deuce, Ademar, and a teary, ten-year-old Anil over his father's shoulder. Dell City was a ridiculously improbable terrorist target, but so the Pentagon had been just a few hours earlier, so the principal had decided to call off school for the day. Like moms and dads throughout the country, Dell City parents had rushed to gather their kids from school after the attack, sitting them down at home and struggling to explain what had happened. Solomons knew Jack was in Denver discussing legal strategies with Dell City stakeholders for their upcoming case on domain over the liquid gold in the Bone Springs–Victorio Peak Aquifer. Denver might have been a target on 9/11, and Solomons had a quick word with Crockett.

"Heard from Jack?"

"Yeah, he's fine. Ready to fight, as always. Fretting a little over how it might affect markets, and his water deal."

"How's that going?"

"Off the record, Andrew, this one could end up in Austin, Supreme Court. And he won't be making any friends around here if it cuts his way."

"What about you, Tam? Ali, Sana—everybody okay?"

"All good, Andrew, appreciate you asking. At least as

good as it could be for a Muslim family in West Texas after that shit in New York."

"Hell, we're all Americans, Texans."

"Whatever that means."

Crockett opened the door for the kids and whispered in Tam's ear as he walked by. "Shit, my mom's in New York."

Bitsy's body, somewhere under the smoldering ruins of the Twin Towers, was never found, and the Laws held out hope for a few days that she might turn up. But Eula knew, particularly after she found Bitsy's diary with all the sordid details of her affair with Jeffrey Lyons. Eula concocted a credible story about how Bitsy had planned to see a UT friend who worked at Cantor Fitzgerald, and a few scraps of forensic evidence emerged over the weeks that seemed to confirm she died in the attack. But Ray, who pored over UT yearbooks and old frat house photographs, never quite bought that story. It ate at him—not because he really cared that much for Bitsy but because he'd never gotten the last word.

President Bush had been sitting in the front of a classroom of second graders at the Emma E. Booker Elementary School in Sarasota, Florida—a kids' book in his lap like a father preparing to read a bedtime story—when Chief of Staff Andrew Card leaned over and whispered into his ear, "America is under attack." Saddam Hussein's invasion of Kuwait had been the defining moment of his father's presidency, and 9/11 would be his.

At 8:30 that evening, Bush, behind his mahogany desk in a somber black suit, addressed the nation from the Oval Office.

"Today, our fellow citizens, our way of life, our very freedom came under attack in a series of deliberate and deadly terrorist acts. . . . These acts of mass murder were intended to frighten our nation into chaos and retreat. But they have failed. Our country is strong. . . . Tonight I ask for prayers for all those who grieve, for the children whose worlds have been shattered, for all whose sense of safety and security has been threatened. And I pray they will be comforted by a power greater than any of us, spoken through the ages in Psalm 23: *Even though I walk through the valley of the shadow of death, I fear no evil for you are with me.*"

CHAPTER 2

Jack Laws had one enduring memory from his meeting in Denver that day with the wildcatter who had bought thirty-five thousand acres of farmland nearly two decades ago, and it had nothing to do with 9/11. When he sat down in the fancy conference room on the twenty-fourth floor of the Anaconda Towers, there were four framed black-and-white photographs, three feet square, of water gushing from pipes on a farm. Jack laughed to himself. Marcie had been right—he'd been looking for water "from the get-go." Marcie was always right.

Meanwhile, Marcie was finishing up two days of meeting with El Paso officials and had shaken hands over a deal to sell the rights for ten million dollars worth of water, the beginning of an endgame for the Laws that could net them ten times that much money in a decade. But there was a catch, a potentially fatal flaw in their strategy that could blow up the whole deal, and, uncharacteristically, a misjudgment of trust.

At the root of their problem was Winfield Edelman, an Austin attorney who had a history of working with water utilities and a reputation for doing whatever it took to shape the Texas Legislature in favor of a client, even if that meant bending the rules or buttering up a congressman with Cuban cigars and the occasional high-priced escort. At $500 an hour,

Edelman had helped the Laws come up with the underlying strategy for their water play, beginning with the Denver group buying their land and the Laws easing out of farming altogether over two decades. Under that plan, the Laws would retain rights to as much water as they could pump from the Bone Springs–Victorio Peak Aquifer and shed the endless headaches of farming in the high desert of West Texas. Edelman knew the science and politics of water in Texas, having worked for several utilities in his early years before earning a law degree at a local night school. Right of capture, which entitled landowners to as much water as they could pump, was the law of the land in Texas, and based on that, Edelman assured the Laws that they were sitting on a goldmine.

"Slam dunk," Edelman told Marcie over pork-cheek quesadillas and dirty martinis in the bar at the Driskill Hotel in Austin, and he extended his hand for a ceremonial fist bump.

Marcie was no stranger to those silly male-bonding rituals, but she felt put off by Edelman's oily confidence. "What?"

"It's a basketball thing."

"Oh. What if the law changes?"

"Trust me, it won't."

Nobody knew Edelman was playing all ends against the middle, working with two other large Texas farming concerns and a group of smallholder farmers pushing for a change in the rules that could bring down the Laws' house of cards. They knew full well what the land barons had up their sleeves and were concerned that thirsty major Texas cities would pump the aquifers dry, leaving them with land where nothing but cactus and mesquite could grow. The concerns of the smallholder farmers, representing thousands of votes across the state, were no secret, and fists had flown on more than one occasion at heated city council meetings. They were pushing wherever they could to amend the law in a way that limited water rights to an average of what was used during a ten-year period, which would cut the legs out from under big landowners like the Laws who had all but stopped farming with an eye toward selling water instead. And the gerrymandering of water districts, particularly in West Texas, had made it even more complicated.

Everyone lawyered up when the law was changed in 2003, in a cluster of cases that would eventually be decided by the Texas Supreme Court.

All Edelman wanted was a plate of Tex-Mex and a few Coronas at Rosa's Cantina, the iconic hole-in-the-wall immortalized in Marty Robbins's 1959 country classic, "El Paso." After the law was changed, Edelman had received some threats—phone calls, slashed tires, and the like—but he figured it would be safe for one last meal at the nondescript cantina on Doniphan Avenue east of downtown El Paso before heading to Austin. Being Tuesday, the Don Haskins Special was the featured dish, and Edelman had a craving for the lump of Mexican-style meat loaf, mashed potatoes, corn, and Spanish rice. He sat in a corner under a racy 1950s-era poster of a busty pinup gal in a bathing suit and sombrero sitting seductively on a wooden fence thumbing a ride down some deserted West Texas highway.

Edelman was feeling pretty good about his grifting after the meal and two shots of Don Julio and sung a few lines from that old Marty Robbins song while walking with a cocky swag to his black Cadillac El Dorado. "Out in the West Texas town of El Paso, I fell in love with a Mexican girl." Edelman unlocked the Caddy. "Nighttime would find me in Rosa's Cantina, music would play and . . ." He stopped singing as a vile smell poured from the open car door. A disemboweled skunk lay across the dashboard, with a note hanging from the blade of a knife stuck in its chest. "Just keep driving." Edelman felt Rosa's meat loaf and mashed potatoes surge through his bowels as he fumbled with the keys, and some of that cream gravy seeped into his boxers with the crack of a rifle and a dull thud into the side of his car. He was out of the parking lot in no time, but not before another bullet hit a few inches from the first.

Edelman never told anyone about it. But he dug out the slugs and took them to a gun expert in Austin, who told him they were from a 30.30. That was his last visit to El Paso.

CHAPTER 3

HUDSPETH COUNTY HERALD
BURR UNDER MY SADDLE
A Forum for Anonymous Commentary
from County Residents

A brittle optimism has begun to emerge in the United States after the nightmare of 9/11, bolstered by the tenuous allied victory in Iraq and the capture of Saddam Hussein in a dusty spider hole outside the town of ad-Dawr in an operation known as Red Dawn.

But that optimism is nothing like the humble, can-do attitude after World War II. It has an aggressive, inward-facing flavor to it that seems to focus on blame rather than healing.

One symptom of what I'll call a festering American radicalism has manifested in a backlash against Muslims that intensified with 9/11, terrorist attacks in the major capitals of Europe, and the emergence of a violent insurgent group called the Islamic State of Iraq and the Levant. Its leader, a guy named Zarqawi, has made the brutal reign of Saddam look like child's play.

One can't help but see our nation is divided and unable to find equilibrium. Every passing day, every terrorist attack, every decapitated body on the doorstep of an Iraqi home undermines the brazen "Mission Accomplished" banner that hung behind President Bush on the USS *Abraham Lincoln* during his victory speech off the coast of San Diego. Societies under siege look for someone to blame, and there is no better scapegoat in the United States than Muslim Americans.

We don't scapegoat our neighbors in Dell City.

CHAPTER 4

Anil was small for a fourteen-year-old boy, and he never strayed too far from Ademar, his twin sister and guardian. He was immature for his age, not even close to the surging hormones of puberty, and enjoyed nothing more than playing hide-and-seek with younger kids in Dell City.

Ademar had one eye on her book and one eye on Anil and his friends as she studied geography in the front porch shade of her parents' house on the Zarkan family compound, just within the boundaries of the Laws' farm. It was not unusual for these games to end with Anil in tears, but something about this particular episode—with Anil on the ground surrounded by three laughing boys—looked different. Ademar strode across the yard and waded into the cluster.

"What's going on?"

The largest of the three boys looked at her defiantly. "We're playing cowboys and Muslims."

Ademar turned to look at the other two boys, eyes on the ground and kicking dirt, then to Anil at her feet with streaks of dirt and tears on his cheeks. She spun around quickly and struck like a snake, whipping the biggest boy across the cheek with the first two knuckles of her clenched fist.

"You ain't playing no fucking cowboys and Muslims around here."

Deuce snapped the football to himself, faked a handoff to an imaginary running back, and looped to the left in a wide arc, planting his foot, then firing a 30-yard strike to Crockett in the left corner of the end zone. A few yards upfield, Tam drilled T2 on the nuances of linebacker play, whether to initiate a blitz on an opposing lineman with a spin move or a bull rush. They were rising freshmen at Dell City High School, and this would be their first year on the varsity. The two best friends must have read Solomons's article about their fathers' state championship victory over the Jayton Jayhawks a hundred times and had replayed the best moments during epic knee football games in the Laws' carpeted basement.

These types of summer drills on the dusty field at Dell City High School in the early evening of a West Texas summer reminded Tam and Crockett of more innocent days, before Medina Ridge, before 9/11. Thousands of young men, from one end of Texas to the other, were going through the same ritual, but there was one difference on this particular day in Dell City. They weren't all young men.

Ademar, Deuce, and T2 had been like the three musketeers their entire lives, and it was not uncommon for people to mistake them for three boys, at least until the curves of a woman began to show on Ademar's lithe frame. Other than that obvious difference, she could outrun them and hold her own wrestling, snapping a headlock on the boys that held like a steel bear trap. The boys were strong, but Ademar was smart, always coming up with some clever, elegant solution to a problem. But she couldn't play football, and that really stuck in her craw. That all changed when she discovered her soccer skills could translate to the football field. She trained secretly that summer, with Anil holding the ball for hours on the tee while Ademar drilled it through the goalpost. She was determined not to be the third wheel as Deuce and T2 prepared for the most important event of their young lives—varsity football tryouts.

Tam was the first to notice that Ademar was wearing cleats as she and Anil walked on the field at the high school, and his heart swelled with love at what Almira had told him might be coming. Without a word, Anil and Ademar marched to the other end of the field. Tam, Crockett, Deuce, and T2 stopped what they were doing to watch Anil hold the ball and Ademar split the goalposts—first from the ten, then the twenty, thirty, and finally the forty. Ademar was far from a prideful person, but she felt proud, nothing like a third wheel in their triad when the boys and the men patted her on the back and threw up high fives. Nobody was prouder of her than Deuce, but he felt something else for her, and at fifteen, he wasn't sure what it was.

Barely audible in the distance and above, they could hear the sound of a slow, steady hand-clap and turned to see Coach T descending from the top row of the wooden bleachers. Nobody knew what to expect as he approached.

"Tam, Crockett, boys, good to see you getting in some preseason work." He turned to Ademar. "Looks like you've been doing some practicing too?"

"Yes, sir." Ademar kept her green eyes locked on his, ready to launch into a well-practiced speech on why he should let her play.

"See you at tryouts in three weeks." Then he turned to Tam, with a wink. "Make sure she understands that includes Blood Alley."

After Coach T left the field, Tam yelled, "Zarkan wrestling," and the whole crew crumpled into a heap of headlocks and leg scissors. Within ten seconds, a pitiful whimper floated up from the bottom of the pile, and they untangled, knowing full well that Anil was under there crying.

At first, Ademar was a sideshow during two-a-days, but no one mistreated her—initially out of fear that T2 would whip their ass for anything inappropriate. But with every sprint in the blinding heat, with every push-up, she won their respect as an equal. And everybody, especially Coach T, knew that a sure-footed kicker like Ademar could mean the difference between victory and defeat. It was understood from the beginning that Ademar would only kick, although she held her own in limited contact drills. But a kicker was the last line of defense on a kickoff return, particularly in wide-open six-man ball, and Coach T had to be sure Ademar was up to it. Ademar knew that, as did Tam, Crockett, Deuce, and T2, and they had prepared her the best they could.

The moment of truth, what bullfighters in Juarez call *el momento de la verdad*, came on the final day of summer practice when they lined up for Blood Alley. "Who's up?" Coach T asked, and Javy, the son of Javier Shirley from Tam's and Crockett's high school team, jumped into the middle with a ball. T2, always the first in like his dad, moved toward the center, but Ademar stepped in front of him. "All right then," Coach T said, "on the whistle."

Javy was quick footed, like his dad, and he faked left the moment the whistle blew, hoping Ademar would be thrown off balance and he could slip by her on the right. In her three-point stance, Ademar remembered Tam's advice to "watch their belt buckle; that's where they're going," and she did. The moment Javy cut back right, Ademar was on him, but not with the traditional rock-'em-sock-'em helmet in the chest. She knew that finesse was the only tactic that would prevail against a larger, stronger opponent—something she'd learned working horses—and she stepped slightly to the side of Javy at the moment of collision, throwing her arms around his neck in a classic Zarkan headlock. Physics were on her side, and Javy's feet flew out from under him, landing him flat on his back with a thud that momentarily knocked the air clean out of him. Ademar looked up at T2, who was laughing as he shook his head, then at Deuce, who, oddly enough, felt like hugging her. Coach T smiled. "Well, all right then."

CHAPTER 5

As much as Ademar liked football, the acceptance and intimacy in that "man's club" with Deuce and T2, she loved horses. The power and grace under her was like nothing she had ever experienced, and the deep relationship between human and animal kindled something atavistic inside her that football never could.

With Almira's blessing, Marcie had given Ademar a dapple-gray quarter horse for her eleventh birthday, which she named Ziyada, roughly translated as "the swift one" in Arabic, but she called it simply Z. She spent hours training Z, mostly under the watchful eye of Blue, who, being half herding dog, had a hard time staying on the sidelines. And by the time Z was four, the two of them had made a name for themselves on the high school rodeo circuit. Barrel racing was Ademar's event, and she craved nothing more than that feeling when Z seemed to read her mind, weaving through the three-barrel cloverleaf as if they'd been dancing together for a lifetime.

Rural life in West Texas requires competence with firearms, and Tam had tried to make sure all three of his kids could shoot true. Naturally, Ademar could split a bull's-eye every time at fifty yards with a 30.30, while Anil missed the mark more often than not, even from a prone position. She had killed a few deer, without remorse, but was just as content to stand back and let others take the shot. Ademar relished those days when she, T2, and Deuce would saddle up at dawn for a deer hunt at Rancho Seco, not so much for the hunting as the time spent with her three favorite creatures on the planet.

She enjoyed knitting and cooking with Sana, Bernia, and Almira but never took to the traditional play of other girls in Dell City. Bernia had given Ademar a Barbie doll when she was eight, and had been a little miffed to find it several years later still in the box at the back of her granddaughter's closet. Ademar wore a dress only for those infrequent journeys to the mosque in El Paso and mostly kicked around in jeans, boots, a faded yoke shirt, and a weathered straw cowboy hat. Underneath it all, Ademar was growing into a woman of startling beauty, with sparkling green eyes that, as Ray would say, could "charm the rattle off a rattlesnake." But Deuce, T2, and Anil were the only boys she ever spent any time with, so much so that Almira began to think that Ademar might be a lesbian. Almira had majored in women's studies at UTEP, where she had a number of lesbian friends, and she understood the sexual ambiguities a girl can feel in her teenage years. She would love her only daughter either way but felt a deep need to help her through what could be a confusing time. Almira was not one to beat around the bush and, one evening in the kitchen that summer, approached Ademar on the issue.

"Am I wrong, or did that young man at the mosque catch your eye last week?"

"You're wrong. Not my type."

"Well, what's your type?"

"Dunno, Mom, I don't really think much about it."

Almira took a long pause, stirring some lentils on the stove and checking on pita bread in the oven. "Do you have 'feelings' for boys?"

"I'm not sure what you're getting at, Mom. I like the way I feel around Deuce."

The conversation trailed off, and Almira dropped it. But lying in bed that night, Ademar touched herself in a certain way down there, thinking about what her mother had said.

Ademar and Z were in second place after their first two barrel runs at the Texas High School Rodeo Association Region II finals in Alpine. The leader, local favorite Aliza McRae, four years older, was leading by two full seconds after her third flawless run. Ademar and Z would have to be under fifteen seconds on this third run to win, almost unheard of at the high school level. Ademar pressed her cheek into Z's soft, moist nose, whispering the Muslim prayer for good luck: "O Allah, I beg You to grant me health with faith, faith with good conduct, success followed by further success, mercy and healing, and Your forgiveness and Your satisfaction."

Ademar scratched Z behind the ears, tucked her long pony tail under that old straw cowboy hat, and hopped on the western saddle, worn and stained dark in places with the sweat from years of riding. From the back of the chute for a running start, about forty feet from the entrance to the arena, she could see Deuce leaning over the fence giving her a thumbs-up. Many riders wore spurs to jolt their horses into a sprint within a few strides, but Ademar didn't rely on pain to motivate Z, who was in a full gallop the second he felt pressure on his flanks from the heel of her boots.

Almost a thousand pounds of power surged forward under her as they flew into the arena at nearly twenty-five miles per hour, Deuce and everything else a blur as she focused on the first barrel to the right. They'd done this thousands of time, Z digging his hoofs in after each circle around the plastic barrels and accelerating to the next. They were just under eleven seconds coming around the final turn before the hell-bent-for-leather dash back into the chute when Ademar's boot slipped along Z's moist flank and brushed the barrel. Ademar knew it had been a good run when she spun Z around at the back of the chute, first seeing 14.2 seconds on the timer, then the barrel on its side. She would have been the youngest winner in the history of Texas high school barrel racing and the only Muslim winner of any event from either gender, but the five-second penalty dropped her to fourth. Ademar, deflated, leaned over Z's mane and apologized: *"Ana asif."* I'm sorry.

Ademar was alone in the stall near the back of the arena, brushing Z and cooling him off before the drive home, when the winner, Aliza McRae, walked into the small wooden enclosure.

"Shit luck."

"Thanks, my bad. I screwed it up."

Aliza patted Z on the flank. "Great horse."

"Ziyada, but I call him Z."

"Well, you've got three more years. Glad I don't have to ride against you."

Aliza took her hand from Z's flank and placed it on Ademar's shoulder. She leaned in for what seemed like a sisterly hug, and Ademar leaned in too. As they both raised back up, Aliza paused and kissed Ademar on the lips.

CHAPTER 6

Ademar was off Almira's breast at six months, and Anil officially at one year. But at those times when Anil was inconsolable in the middle of the night, he would reach his tiny hands under her robe, and Almira would allow it. She ended it one morning just past Anil's second birthday when he tossed a sipping cup for milk on the floor and grabbed at her breast. Even without the way Tam looked at her then, Almira knew it was time.

The other kids in Dell City would not tolerate Anil unless he agreed to games where they could torment him in some way: chasing, lassoing, blindfolding, pretend shooting, and the like. He was always tagging along at the heels, or paws, of T2, Deuce, Ademar, and Blue, and everyone knew better than to mess with him when they were around. Tam understood that Anil was different, reconciling himself early on that he wouldn't be a rough-and-tumbler like him or T2, and doted on the child in a way that reassured Almira she had chosen the right man. It frustrated Anil that he could not be the type of son T2 was to Tam, and he cried himself to sleep one night after overhearing his parents talking to Crockett and Lola Mae about their difficulties with him.

Anil adored his great-grandmother, Sana, and like any great-grandmother, she spoiled him rotten. Anil would spend hours at Sana's feet during those knitting sessions with Bernia and Almira, learning the craft from them and absorbing every word of Arabic. Anil would never forget that feeling of pride when Sana framed a patch of cloth he had knitted and hung it over the fireplace in the living room. He never missed the chance to accompany her on visits to the mosque in El Paso, where everybody accepted him and he could join in a communal activity with no fear of scorn or bullying. But giving Anil a Mac PowerBook for his fourteenth birthday, as something of a consolation for all the attention T2 and Ademar were receiving by playing football, was the single most influential thing Sana would ever do for him.

The web opened up a world for Anil where he could be anyone or anything he wanted, where any question would be answered without ridicule, and where he could find friends from every corner of the world who didn't care whether he played football, rode horses, wet his bed, or prayed to Allah. He had finally found something he could do better than anyone else, particularly in a digitally challenged place like Dell City, and he felt a smug superiority over all those classmates and adults asking him for help with projects requiring a graph, posters, PowerPoint or other content he could conjure from his Mac. But it didn't take long for him to be drawn into the dark corners of the web. Anil would spend hours alone in his room playing Grand Theft Auto and, once he was sure everyone was asleep, masturbating in private shame to pornographic videos of women he began to think of as girlfriends.

It was during one of those late-night sessions toggling between Ass Parade and Grand Theft Auto: Liberty City Stories, where his avatar was weaving a souped-up motorcycle through an urban chase, that he received a request to meet Larry of Arabia in a chatroom. He followed a complicated digital trail through the backdoor maze of the popular video game and found a hyperlink that Larry of Arabia said he should "check out." The link opened to a video of a thin, pious-looking Muslim with a beard, skullcap, and glasses who, Anil would discover later, was a Yemeni American named Anwar al-Alwlaki from Las Cruces, New Mexico, 135 miles northwest of Dell City. Al-Alwlaki spoke in Arabic, which Anil understood, and what the cleric had to say simultaneously repulsed and fascinated him in the same way as those videos of naked blond women rubbing oil on their privates.

"Don't consult with anybody in the killing of Americans. Fighting the devil doesn't require consultation or prayers seeking divine guidance. They are the party of the devils. Fighting them is what is called for at this time. We have reached a point where it is either us or them. We are two opposites that will never come together. What they want can only be accomplished by our elimination. Therefore, this is a defining battle. These kings, emirs, and presidents are not qualified to lead this nation. They are not even qualified to lead a flock of sheep, let alone a nation of over one billion Muslims."

Anil would watch that video dozens of times over the next week. But on this night, it made him think about President Bush, Governor Rick Perry, and why every morning the high school required them to recite the Pledge of Allegiance and the Texas version with one hand over their hearts. "Honor the Texas flag. I pledge allegiance to thee, Texas, one state under God, one and indivisible."

CHAPTER 7

Before 9/11 and the cancer of violent extremism that metastasized in the late 1990s, terrorism had been largely viewed as the domain of a few well-known Middle Eastern brands—Hezbollah, Islamic jihad, and Hamas—or of state sponsors in Libya and Iran. American and European intelligence agencies were caught off guard by the emergence of a powerful new cadre of groups like al-Qa'ida and individuals like al-Alwaki. But the world changed late on the night of June 25, 1996, when a powerful truck bomb sheared off the front half of Khobar Towers, an eight-story building in eastern Saudi Arabia housing US Air Force personnel enforcing a no-fly zone over Iraq, killing twenty and injuring almost five hundred.

President Clinton's secretary of state, Warren Christopher, and his inner circle of advisors were ending another shuttle mission to narrow differences between Israel, Syria, Lebanon, Jordan, and the Palestinians over a comprehensive peace. Most of these missions included stops in Saudi Arabia for consultations with King Abdullah and Foreign Minister Faisal on the status of negotiations, or to press them on bilateral issues like the price of oil and the purchase of some high-dollar American weapons system. Saudi Arabia, home to the most revered sites in Islam, Mecca and Medina, was tightly controlled by the royal family and seemingly immune to terrorist attack. And a strike on territory at the heart of Islam was the last story Christopher's small traveling press corps expected to be chasing as they sat in the lobby of a Saudi royal guest palace sipping Turkish coffee, playing liar's poker, and waiting for an update from spokesman Nicholas Burns.

As always, the Associated Press's Barry Schweid led the bidding with the subset of reporters who were not nodding off on one of the lush couches, joined by CNN's Steve Hurst, ABC's John McWethy, Reuters's Carol Giacomo, Agence France-Presse's Andre Viollaz, and United Press International's Sid Balman. Burns, accompanied by Saudi Arabia's powerful former US ambassador, Prince Bandar bin Sultan, might as well have tossed a cobra into the lobby when he dropped the news about the bombing and instructed the press corps to board a bus for a visit to the decimated site. The Saudis—hypersensitive to any type of media coverage, much less the no-holds-barred style of the Western press—were in a pickle. A major news event with deep international ramifications had dropped into the lap of a seasoned press corps traveling with a distinguished American official, whose State Department regularly raked the Saudis over the coals about press freedom. Christopher, a skilled attorney, savvy diplomat, and advocate behind the scenes for human rights, had secured permission from the king for the press visit to Khobar Towers and a briefing from Bandar. When Bandar said they "thought" this might be the work of a group linked to al-Qa'ida, it was the first time the veteran press corps and the editors they phoned their stories in to had heard of the terrorist organization. But it would not be the last, not by a long shot.

Al-Qa'ida and its Rasputinesque leader, Osama bin Laden, preached a hybrid form of Wahhabi Islam that interprets the Qur'an literally and considers those who don't follow their way as heathens and enemies. Wahhabism is the dominant strain of Islam in Saudi Arabia, where bin Laden was born to a Yemeni immigrant who built a vast fortune in the construction business due in large part to close ties with the royal family. Well educated at the most elite Saudi schools, including King Abdulaziz University, bin Laden grew increasingly radicalized in his view that the big Western powers and the Soviet Union treated Muslims as colonial subjects. He made a name for himself against the Soviets on the battlefields of Afghanistan, funneling millions of dollars in materiel to the Mujahidin. He founded al-Qa'ida in 1988 from his base in Saudi Arabia, which viewed bin Laden as an internal threat and banished him four years later under heavy pressure from the Western allies.

Relocating to Sudan, bin Laden commanded a decentralized, diverse global terrorist organization that took asymmetric warfare against Western targets to a new level of destruction and precision, including the near-simultaneous bombings of US embassies in Kenya and Tanzania, a small-scale bombing of the World Trade Center in 1993, a suicide bombing of the USS *Cole*, and the catastrophic attacks of 9/11. He found common ground with the Taliban in Afghanistan, where he thumbed his nose at the United States while playing a cat-and-mouse game with allied forces after the invasion following 9/11. With intelligence agencies and special forces tracking his every move, both online and off, and the emergence of ISIS in Iraq, bin Laden became marginalized and limited to an occasional threatening video from his hiding place in a residence a few miles down the road from a Pakistani military base near the northern town of Abbottabad. It was there that Navy Seals and CIA special operators took him down during a daring nighttime raid ordered by President Barack Obama. Hard drives and thumb discs seized at the residence revealed that bin Laden had a taste for video games and Western pornography.

Following the killings of bin Laden and Anwar al-Alwlaki by a US drone strike in Yemen, ISIS inherited the mantle as the standard-bearer for the war against the West. The group's ideology centered on Salafism, considered a purer form of Sunni Islam, and ISIS militarized its tactics in a way that crept up on the Western allies and on Obama, who once referred to them as the "junior varsity." Far from being a junior varsity, ISIS created its "caliphate" by seizing large chunks of territory in Iraq and Syria with a brutality unseen since the Middle Ages and a sophistication with the internet to rival the geekiest coders in Long Island City or Bangalore. Its propaganda, including magazines, videos, and animations pulsing through almost every social media channel, was as good as anything coming out of the slickest ad agencies in New York or London. And through the web, it radicalized thousands of recruits among the disenchanted youth in such unlikely places as Minneapolis; Brussels; Paris; and Birmingham, England—promising them a place in heaven with seventy-two virgins if they chose martyrdom under their black flag. ISIS-led operations were potent and brutal in the Middle East—slaughtering entire villages in a single day and, in one particularly shocking murder captured on a professionally produced video, incinerating a captured Jordanian pilot in a steel cage. ISIS-inspired attacks, enabled through propaganda and virtual seminars in the dark corners of the web, shook the West to its foundation in places thought to be untouchable, like Madrid, Quebec, Brussels, and Orlando.

The United States, the United Kingdom, and the European Union created a virtual cottage industry among private firms in a new set of web-based tactics to counter violent extremism. And under increasing pressure from governments to cooperate against terrorism, firms like Google, Facebook, and Twitter began partnering with traditional international development contractors and communications firms to develop strategies that might counter violent extremism. The US Departments of State, Defense, and Homeland Security, the CIA, and their sister organizations in the UK funneled hundreds of millions of dollars in contracts to private firms in Washington and London, who in turn partnered with social media concerns, advertising agencies, and universities to spend taxpayer money on research or theoretical approaches to "CVE." These consortiums rolled out page after page of white papers on their success working with at-risk communities through intellectually questionable diagnostic tools and development-based programs they claimed could successfully counter violent extremists. But they failed miserably in providing the one thing governments sought: the ability to identify and thwart the lone-wolf terrorist or deeply embedded terrorist cell in unlikely locations like Dell City.

With Syria and Iraq in tatters, dangerous big-power alliances emerging, and a shocking anti-Muslim bias coursing through the United States and Europe, fueled by the rhetoric of politicians like Donald Trump and France's Marie Le Pen, Washington unleashed the military on ISIS. Although it took some time to gain traction, drones, air strikes, and special operations were able to turn the tide against the violent extremist organization. But they couldn't kill them all, and like when an insecticide bomb goes off in an infested apartment, the cockroaches fled elsewhere by the hundreds. Pouring into the Middle East, the Balkans, Europe, and, in fewer numbers, the United States, the foreign fighters would surrender themselves to authorities for brief prison sentences. The ISIS warriors, both men and women, would bide their time in prison radicalizing fellow inmates and planning operations to carry out once they were released into their communities. Working with these inmates proved another solid revenue stream for the private firms with their CVE practice areas and their costly theories, costlier still in the field.

CHAPTER 8

Anil had become increasingly withdrawn and taciturn in the two years since his initial contact with Larry of Arabia, who had plugged him into a network of virtual friends that fed his growing interest in all things Muslim and connected him to Cleo the Leo, who looked like a carefree Muslim girl in London. She introduced him to a new social networking tool called Twitter, and used it to send him a photograph of her with only a scarf over her hair and an imprint of a red lipstick kiss superimposed on the side.

She also urged him to stand up for himself against some of the bullying at school that he whined about to her after two boys snatched his beloved laptop and hid it behind the gym when T2, Deuce, and Ademar weren't around. Her last direct Tweet to him that night—"What would your John Wayne do?"—was on his mind the next day when one of the boys taunted him during lunch about removing pork from his cafeteria sandwich. Seething, and with images in his mind's eye of that scene at the end of *True Grit* when John Wayne squares off for a heroic shootout against four desperadoes, Anil removed everything from his steel lunch tray and waited for the right moment. When the boy looked away, Anil slashed him across the face with the edge of the tray, opening a red line across his cheek that exposed white bone for a moment before blood filled it and dripped down his neck to the floor. Dell City High School had its share of fights, mostly the innocent schoolyard dustups that ended in a headlock, but the ferocity of this sudden attack stunned the lunchroom into silence. The principal marched Anil to the office, calling Almira to pick him up and not to bring him back for the rest of the week.

Almira and Lola Mae often ended the day chatting over a cup of tea on one of their front porches while Crockett and Tam sat inside discussing the latest goings-on with the farm or some development in the sports world. Almira held her cup between her knees, wanting to say something but not sure how to start. Lola Mae had a sixth sense about human nature, about feelings—always scooping one of their children into her arms when they were young at exactly the moment before a crisis and making them forget about whatever little drama was about to dissolve them into tears. She could sense that Almira's sniffing was about something more than allergies and placed a hand on her friend's knee.

"Just let it out, Almira."

"It's Anil. He injured a boy today in a fight. He had to get fifteen stitches."

"Did he deserve it?"

"I don't know, teasing or some such. But it's more than that. He's so withdrawn—stays up so late with that computer. Tam says it's just a teenage phase, but I don't know."

When Tam heard his name, he and Crockett came out to the porch.

"What's up, are you crying?"

"Almira was telling me about Anil's fight at school today . . . you know, the computer and everything else."

Tam always had an answer when life threw them some small-time curveball with the kids, but this was clearly a pitch that he had no idea how to swing at. Crockett, trained at West

Point to be an infantry officer who could connect all the dots and come up with a solution, had a suggestion they all liked.

"Put him on the crew with Tam and me this summer. We can keep an eye on him, try to figure this all out. The hard work will be good for him. He'll make some money, build those muscles, and learn something that a computer can't teach. T2 and Deuce are doing it too."

With so much time by himself as a child, Anil would spend hours building intricate societies out of LEGOs and navigating through them with his impressive collection of toy vehicles. The crown jewels of Anil's collection were the farm machines he pushed around in a few handfuls of dirt, pretending to farm the land around his LEGO creations. When they were a little older, T2, Deuce, and Ademar would rush to the equipment sheds after dinner to scramble around on the tractors that picked, baled, and processed cotton, long green chilies, tomatoes, onions, and cantaloupes. As farm kids, they knew how dangerous the equipment could be, and Blue would remind them with a bark or a nip when one of them was doing something risky. Deuce and T2 had worked in the fields the past two summers, but Anil, as usual, was left behind. When Tam offered him a spot alongside them that summer, Anil saw it as anything but a punishment in his distorted way of thinking, more like an invitation into the men's club after proving himself by decking that kid at school. Anil had stayed up late again with his virtual friends on the web the night before his first day on the job, but Almira was pleased to see him first at the table for breakfast. Anil looked every inch a farmhand, in miniature, and Almira told him as delicately as possible that one of his bootlaces was untied.

Anil's main tasks the first month involved riding in the cabs of harvesters or tillers doing whatever little task came up: lugging tools around, adjusting sprinklers on the center-pivot irrigator, and cleaning up at the end of the day. Anil didn't mind the long days in the dust, heat, and wind, and most nights he fell into bed without a peek into the cyber world where he had spent almost every free moment the past few years. Baby fat began to give way to real muscles—he was a Zarkan after all—and Tam chuckled when Anil pulled his shirt up one morning to show off his abs.

As summer spooled out, Anil took on increasingly more difficult jobs, and by August he was allowed to stand on the front of the massive chili harvester helping Deuce and T2 pull out any debris that might jam the conveyer. It could be a dangerous job, requiring balance and attention to avoid being tangled while freeing anything stuck in the belt. Anil caught on quickly, almost too quickly, and T2 had yanked him back roughly from the conveyer one afternoon when his brother was leaning too far over the deck in front of the driver. "Sorry, Anil, but you can't fuck around out here." Anil had reverted to his old pouty self for the rest of the day and complained that night about it to Cleo the Leo in a private chat session on a social networking site called Facebook. Cleo had felt Anil slipping away the past few months and took the opportunity in his moment of vulnerability to reset the hook. "Football guy trying to keep a brother down. Not the Muslim way."

Anil seemed to have shaken it off the next morning as he stood next to Deuce on the deck of the chili harvester, with Tam in the cab learning how to drive the picker. Anil was the first to reach for some type of long stalk stuck in the conveyer just as the picker jerked over a mound of dirt, knocking Anil to his knees with his right hand dangling inches away from the spinning machinery. Deuce made a desperate grab for Anil's belt, likely saving his life but not his hand. Deuce pulled Anil to his feet and back against the cab, the ragged stump that had once been his hand slamming against the windshield in front of T2 and smearing it with blood. The driver and the two boys stanched the bleeding as best they could with a tourniquet from the first aid kit and phoned it in to the main house. A helicopter from Providence Hospital in El Paso was waiting in front of the Laws's house when they returned from the field.

Anil woke up in a hospital bed with all the Laws and Zarkans crowded around, his twin Ademar holding the one hand he still had. Anil looked through a narcotic haze at his gauzed stump, then at Ademar. "I won't be able to hold the football for you anymore."

Ademar didn't have any tears left when she and Deuce stood in the elevator. She sensed that he had something to say.

"I'm sorry, Addie."

She turned and stepped close to him. "It's not your fault, Deuce. You saved his life. I'm grateful you were there."

Ademar had never seen a man cry, except in movies or on television, and the single tear that formed on Deuce's eyelash and ran slowly down his cheek touched something in her that she didn't know was there. Ademar cupped Deuce's face in both hands, pulled him down to her, and kissed the tear gently away.

CHAPTER 9

By the time Deuce and T2 were seniors at Dell City High in 2007, they had made a name for themselves in Texas schoolboy football. They had followed in the footsteps of their fathers, Deuce a rangy gunslinging quarterback and T2 the monster of the midway at middle linebacker. The population of Dell City had shrunk considerably since their fathers' youth, to about five hundred, and the quality of the other players on Coach T's squad was nothing like two decades ago. But they had what Coach T called his "secret weapon," Ademar and her "magic toe," which wasn't such a secret after three years of counting on her to win games that often hinged on a last-second field goal.

T2 and Deuce were also following in their fathers' footsteps when it came to plans for playing at the next level, with West Point and UTEP their probable landing spots.

Deuce's official visit to West Point was bittersweet on several levels, dredging up suspicions about the reasons for Bitsy's whereabouts on 9/11 and resurrecting all the conflicting feelings surrounding Crockett's military experience. No doubt, Eula cracked one evening around the Laws' firepit, if Bitsy had been around, she would have accompanied Deuce and insisted on staying in the Douglas MacArthur suite at the Thayer Hotel. The head coach, a giant of a man who had played tackle in the NFL for fifteen years and won a Super Bowl with the San Diego Chargers, led Deuce and Crockett through the West Point dog-and-pony show, which had the predictable impact on Deuce. Crockett kept his ambivalence to himself, not wanting to rain on his son's parade, but his thoughts kept returning to Medina Ridge and feelings about the ambiguities of military service as the coach led them around Trophy Point, the Plain, and Grant Hall. The Laws had built up an impressive roster of friends among the Texas political elite, and Governor Rick Perry had taken a shine to Eula, at least enough of one to wrangle a West Point nomination for Deuce from the congressional delegation in Washington. There was no question in Deuce's mind, and he accepted the coach's offer on the spot.

Almira's biggest concern about T2 playing at UTEP centered around the head coach, who had been fired the previous year at Alabama over allegations of visiting a strip club in Florida. Tam shared his wife's feelings on the issue, and neither of them pulled any punches in their questioning of the coach. Like Crockett, they didn't want to take the wind out of T2's sails, who had hoped for a full scholarship but settled for the same deal as his father—preferred walk-on with vague promises of a scholarship if he performed as well at eleven-man ball as he did at six-man.

T2 and Deuce were set by the time the last regular-season game rolled around in November.

The Cougars would have to beat the Marfa Shorthorns to qualify for the six-man championships in early December, and everyone seemed to be wearing T-shirts with a clever graphic Anil had designed late one night on his computer: Z^2 + Deuce = Victory. It was a rare appearance at the breakfast table from Anil, unshaven and unwashed after an all-nighter in cyberspace, and his being there, caring enough to make the T-shirt design and present it to them that morning, gave the family a brief glimmer of hope after what had been a dark three years for the boy since the accident.

The week prior to the last game of the season was a fun time for the students, with pep rallies and preparations for the senior prom after the game, which would be in an abandoned cotton mill just out of town that was being fashioned into a Texas dance hall for the party. T2, Deuce, and Ademar were focused on the game and hadn't given it much thought until they dropped by to help the prom decorations subcommittee at the mill. The neatly stacked hay bales, the flags, the lights, and a dance floor in front of the stage raised the obvious question about whether, and with whom, they would go.

The relationship between Deuce and Ademar had ripened over the years, accelerated by the affection she'd shown for him in the elevator at the hospital after Anil's accident. They were close, but the physical side of it remained absolutely platonic. With some help on the computer from Anil, Deuce had put time into understanding the traditions and rules of Islam and had learned enough to know that any type of advance toward Ademar could put him on thin ice. Even dancing could be considered *haram*, forbidden under the Qur'an, although there is a brief mention of it as tolerable under chaste circumstances in the second most important book for Muslims, the Hadith. Ademar had strong feelings for Deuce and erotic thoughts she had discussed with Almira, erasing any doubts from a few years back about her daughter's sexuality. Almira trusted Ademar, knew what a nonstarter it would be to lecture her on Islamic rules, and counseled her daughter to "be patient and let nature take its course."

The question of attending the dance hung in the air of the pickup cab as the three of them drove back to Dell City from the prom site. T2, always the practical problem solver, who loved both of them, came up with a solution he was sure nobody would object to.

"How about a triple date—the three of us?"

Deuce turned toward Ademar between them in the truck. "Can you?"

Ademar laughed in the affectionate way a woman might at an innocent, obvious question from a child and placed her hand on Deuce's knee for just a moment. "Yes."

As usual, the game against Marfa came down to the final seconds, Cougars down by a point on the Shorthorns 25-yard line, and Ademar began trotting onto the field before Coach T could give her the nod. Every person in the stadium was on their feet by the time Ademar signaled for the snap to the holder, Deuce, who at that moment would not have trusted the outcome of what could be the final game of his high school career to anyone else in the world. But there would be no heroic ending. The center hiked the ball over Deuce's head and a Shorthorn pounced on it as the clock wound down to zero.

Ademar felt better by the time she made it back to the house that afternoon, where all the Zarkan and Laws women were waiting for her with what they hoped would be a pleasant surprise, and a taste of what it meant to be a high school junior on prom night. Eula had arranged with Donnie Ziler to reserve all his time for them at the Cut and Curl Beauty Shop, the only salon for a hundred miles. The closest thing Ademar had ever come to a professional hairdo was when Sana or Bernia would twist her long, dark hair into a braid, and she knew there was no way of balking gracefully at the full treatment from Donnie. One by one he coifed the eight women: Marcelina, Eula, Lola Mae, India, Sana, Bernia, Almira, and, finally, Ademar. Donnie was a maestro, a whirling dervish of beauty—washing, clipping, brushing, and adjusting temperatures on the two old-style driers as he lowered the plastic space-helmet attachments down over their heads. "Best for last," Donnie said to Ademar, and, as one, the seven women lowered their *People* magazines and *Hudspeth County Heralds* to watch the transformation of the only girl of that generation among the two families. When it was over, a touch of makeup dabbed on her cheeks and around her green eyes, Donnie stood back, facing the ladies with his arms stretched out like a symphony conductor who had just completed a virtuoso performance. "Voila." Ademar did not recognize the woman staring back at her in the mirror.

And Deuce didn't recognize Ademar either when he picked her up for the prom that evening. "Steady, bro," T2 said as his friend struggled for words at the door. "You're supposed to give her that bluebonnet." The flower floated like an azure island when Ademar pinned it on her dark green linen dress, conservatively styled with long sleeves, a boat neck, and a hemline just above her ankles. Donnie opted against anything that would leave Ademar's hair stiff or unnatural—upswept loosely with thick braids around it and a few strands falling out in a way that emphasized her casual beauty. Sana's silver hair brooch with two small turquoise ladybugs, a family heirloom almost the same color as Ademar's eyes, held it all together. Crockett could hardly believe that just a few hours ago this woman had been lining up to kick a field goal in black cleats, sweaty shoulder pads, and a football helmet.

It was one of those nights in the life of a young person that brings into sharp granularity all that came before it, and all that would follow.

They danced together at first as a trio, spinning and dipping with their arms around each other, laughing at their toe-mashing awkwardness as the music played and moths gathered around the flickering lamps. T2 stepped back near the end of the dance as the band began a series of slow, romantic songs, starting with Alan Jackson's "Remember When." Deuce and Ademar moved closer to each other as if they had been dancing together for a lifetime, her lips so near his ear that he could hear her breathe. They both knew the moment was fragile, and they held it with open hands lest it break into a hundred tiny pieces that they could never reassemble. When the music stopped, they pulled apart slowly and rested their foreheads together. The smell of her lilac perfume hung in the air between them, and Deuce wanted to kiss her but did not.

The three of them drove back to the farm in the pickup, and for an awkward moment in front of the Zarkan house, nobody quite knew what to do. T2, the third wheel for the first time in a friendship that had begun in the crib, broke the ice.

"Great night, you two. I'm heading in. See you tomorrow."

"I'll be there in a bit. There's something I want to give Deuce."

They all knew every inch of Hudspeth County, but there was something Ademar wanted to show Deuce that happened about this time every year at the base of Guadalupe Peak near an embankment overlooking Rancho Seco. They made small talk over the radio during the forty-minute drive, every bump nudging their legs closer. Deuce turned into a small open space on the embankment, and they could see the lights of Dell City in the distance. But there was something else, what looked like dozens of tiny diamonds, almost close enough to touch, shimmering in the headlamps of the truck. Ademar had seen them once before with Tam and knew what they were.

"Deer." They were bedded down for the night in the warmth captured at the base of the mountains. "Quiet, let's get in the back so we can see them better."

Hay bales from the parade before the prom lined the walls of the truck bed, and blankets to keep the riders warm were pushed together in the middle. Ademar and Deuce pulled the blankets around them as they sat with their backs to the cab.

"Ademar, I . . ." She put her finger on Deuce's lip to stop him.

"I actually have two gifts for you. This," Ademar said, holding an outstretched arm to the field.

"Something else."

"Yes." And she kissed him on the lips. "And this."

Ademar removed the turquoise ladybug brooch, and her hair fell around her shoulders. She slid out of her dress, pulling the blankets closer around them, kissing Crockett underneath each piece of his clothing that she removed. Their bodies wound around each other, and they were as close as two creatures could be, joined under a moonless night with the endless West Texas sky full of stars sparkling over them and a field full of oval gems shimmering in the truck lights before them. It was as if both their Gods, or the one God that each of their faiths interpreted in a different way, had created this private gift for both of them. There would be no judging this perfect moment, Ademar thought, not from her family and not from her God.

CHAPTER 10

Anil was not the only person in Dell City who had a secret life on the web.

Ray Laws seemed to be stumbling through life like a zombie since Bitsy's death, staying up all night with whiskey, meth, and his computer—popping a few oxys just before dawn to sleep. He spent hours reading stories on right-wing websites like Breitbart, the Drudge Report, and Newsmax about 9/11 conspiracy theories, racial purity, and the citizenship of a certain Illinois senator who was running for president. He found a kindred spirit on Stormfront, a white nationalist online community promoting racism and anti-Semitism, in someone going by the pseudonym Lynch 'Em, who had an uncanny knack for poking Ray in just the right place.

The path to radicalization can take many forms, and it's not limited to young Muslims. Ray's life and self-esteem had been taken from him just as surely as Anil's hand had been ripped off by that chili picker. And he thought that the America in which he now lived was run by "liberal Jews and niggers" who had no intention of including him in the socialist panacea he imagined they wanted to create. Jack and Marcie had no sway over their middle-aged son anymore, and Crockett spent as little time as possible with his father after Ray and Orhan nearly came to blows over Deuce's relationship with Ademar, whom he referred to as a "gold digger."

Another late, lonely night in Dell City, and Ray might have made the two-hour trip to Juarez for a whore, but his impotence the past few years, no matter what dosage of Viagra he took, only fueled his rage. Ray stumbled into the Sheepherder's Bar around closing, where a few Latin farmhands on stools were speaking Spanish with Hudspeth County's new deputy sheriff, Ronin Montoya, the son of a Mexican man and a Japanese American woman. Bonnie LaRue, who had presided for almost three decades over the only local watering hole in Dell City, smudged out a Lucky in the ashtray when she saw Ray. Bonnie knew trouble when it walked in the door.

"What can I get you, Ray."

"A place to drink where they speak English, and three fingers of Jack."

Ray spoke loud enough for Montoya and the farmhands to hear him, and they turned around.

"No speaky de English, speaky de spic?" Ray said.

The farmhands slid out of their barstools, fists coiled, but Montoya, an army veteran and no stranger to these kinds of racial flare-ups from his days at the front lines of the second Iraq war, settled them down.

"I'll pay for that drink, Bonnie, then Ray needs to call it a night."

"I'll call it a night when I'm damn ready, deputy *pendejo*."

Montoya put his hand on Ray's shoulder—friendly, firm. "Nobody wants any trouble."

"Then get your fucking hands off me," he said, slapping the deputy's hand off and pushing Montoya on the chest hard enough to knock him back a few feet.

Ray was in no shape to defend himself and was across the bar in handcuffs before he knew what hit him. Eula was not surprised late that night when she received the call from

Montoya to come pick Ray up in jail. "No charge, Eula, but someone needs to drive him home."

Ray slumped next to his sister in the cab of the pickup, a shadow of his former self, gut piled over a ranger belt, cowboy hat almost sideways, and so crippled up by decades of stooping in the fields that he could hardly find a way to sit without pain from his ankles to his neck.

"What the fuck, Ray. You gotta pull out of this."

"What? Just having a little fun."

"Is that what you call fun? Sideways on Jack, puking in jail?"

"Fuck it, Eula. This is America. Those wetbacks need to speak English."

"You're lucky they didn't stick you. Would have if the deputy wasn't there."

"That Jap with a badge? What's he doing in Texas? Probably one of his chink relatives that shot dad's thumb off."

"Cool it, Ray. You need a shrink. There's one in El Paso who did me a lot of good after that rape."

Eula didn't get her last word in before Ray started snoring.

Ray was the first person in line to vote at City Hall on Tuesday, November 4, 2008, wearing a McCain-Palin button, telling anyone who would listen that Barack Obama was a Muslim and a foreigner. He'd been up all night in cyberspace, drinking Jack, snorting meth, and cruising his favorite sites. When he pulled the curtain behind him in the voting booth, he could hardly read the ballot and mistakenly checked the box for Obama, which he noticed just as the card slipped into the slot of the sealed wooden chest.

"Hey. Wait a minute," Ray said, broken blood vessels popping out like crimson spiderwebs around his nose.

"Is there a problem?" asked the clerk, an older woman whose bluish hair could have only been the work of Donnie Ziler.

"I checked the wrong box. Need to change it."

"I'm sorry, we can't open the box."

"Give me that damn thing."

Ray grabbed the box and pulled out a pocket knife to pry it open but stopped when he felt Montoya's hand on his shoulder.

"Back off, Ray, let it be."

"But . . ." and he stopped in midsentence, realizing that word of him voting for Obama would spread like wildfire in Dell City. His head felt like it might explode, his eyes went a little blurry, he felt numb on the left side of his face and was suddenly so tired that he could barely stand.

"Are you okay, Ray? Ray? You better go see a doctor. There's something wrong with your face."

"Fuck it."

Although Ray would never admit to watching CNN, he liked the digital "magic wall" that updated every few minutes with detailed voting results by precinct in every state, and he spent most of the night in a dark bedroom wringing his hands over Wolf Blitzer and John King as the results rolled in. Ray felt weaker as the night wore on, so weary that he could barely keep his eyes open, and nodded off as the map of Texas on the magic wall turned red. When he woke up around midnight, President Obama was delivering his victory speech to a crowd of more than two hundred thousand supporters gathered at Grant Park in Chicago.

". . . We are and always will be the United States of America. . . . It's been a long time coming, but tonight, because of what we did on this date in this election at this defining moment, change has come to America. This is our time, to put our people back to work and open doors of opportunity for our kids; to restore prosperity and promote the cause of peace; to reclaim the American dream and reaffirm that fundamental truth, that out of many, we are one; that while we breathe, we hope. And where we are met with cynicism and doubts and those who tell us that we can't, we will respond with that timeless creed that sums up the spirit of a people: Yes, we can."

Eula was awakened by a gunshot.

She didn't live more than a hundred yards from Ray, and when Eula pulled back the curtains over the window next to the bed, all she saw was the pulsing gray light from a television in his bedroom. Eula knocked on his door, opened it, peeked around the side, walked in, felt her way around furniture and crumpled beer cans to his room. The first thing she noticed was the smell of cigarette smoke and rancid sweat, then Ray, head flopped over the back of a chair and his brains sprayed all over the wall behind him. Ray's arms dangled at his side, a .357 in one hand and a note in the other. Eula could barely read the two words scrawled and falling across the page as if they had been written by a first grader. "Nigger president!"

CHAPTER 11

Ray's suicide was barely a blip on Anil's radar. He didn't like Ray anyway, and the constant wincing pain in his beloved great-grandmother's stomach worried him enough to take a break from his "job" editing anti-American YouTube videos for Cleo the Leo to research what her symptoms might mean. It all pointed to pancreatic cancer, and it was not a big surprise when Ali delivered the news to the family.

"It's not over, Inshallah. The doctor in El Paso is trying to get Sana into an experimental treatment that has shown some good results."

"Inshallah," Orhan, Bernia, Tam, Almira, Ademar, and Anil said at the same time. T2 would have said it too, but he was at UTEP struggling through civil engineering and football.

"But there's a long waiting list. Sana can't get on until insurance approves it."

Pale and withered, Sana doubled over on the couch with another spasm of pain.

"I'll bet she could get on the list if her last name was Jones—or Laws," Anil said, storming into his room and slamming the door.

Before he could fire up the laptop, Anil received notification on his iPhone that a text had come in on a new, encrypted messaging service called WhatsApp, which Cleo the Leo had told him to start using so nobody could snoop on them. Anil transmitted the latest news about Sana, and Cleo, never missing an opportunity to push him further down the road toward jihad, agreed with his read on the situation. "Muslim in America = second-class citizen."

Anil sat with Sana most nights, making sure that not a single part of Islamic ritual was overlooked. Alone with Sana on her final night, he arranged the bed so the soles of her feet faced east toward Mecca and insisted she recite the Shahada, the profession of faith, in preparation for death. "There is no God but Allah, and Muhammad is the messenger of Allah." Those were Sana's final words, heard only by Anil, who closed her eyes and mouth, positioned her head facing east, then woke the women in the family to perform *ghusl*, the ritual washing before mandatory burial within twenty-four hours. Anil made a spectacle of himself at the funeral, wailing and self-flagellating with an ocotillo branch until his back bled, a tradition of an Islamic sect to which the Zarkans did not belong. He wouldn't allow Almira to wash his wounds after the funeral and didn't change clothes or wash for several days. A week later he received a package from Cleo the Leo containing a *taqiyah*, a traditional Muslim skull cap that he wore every day from that point on.

For Ademar, T2, and Deuce, the world had shifted under their feet, each of them orphans in one way or another.

Deuce had shrugged off most of Beast Barracks, those five weeks of hazing at West Point before a plebe's first year officially began, letting it glide over him like water off a duck's back. He missed Ademar and T2 but fell into a familiar routine once he could retreat into the familiar rituals of football, even as a third-string passing quarterback on a team that ran the ball most of the time. But when Crockett called Deuce to tell him about Ray's suicide, it was as if the air had been let out of his life. Sure, he didn't care for what Ray had become, but Ray was still his grandfather, and his profane death shattered Deuce's illusion of what Dell City was to him, the foundation on which he stood in a shifting world. When the commanding officer at West Point, Lieutenant General Franklin Hagenback, summoned Deuce for a meeting, he could barely muster enough energy to shave and put on what he thought would be the appropriate uniform. Hagenback showed genuine concern when he gave Deuce a ticket home for the funeral and provided chauffeured transport to JFK airport. But Deuce found Hagenback's words about family and "stepping up" hollow and irrelevant. As diligent as he was about preparation and attention to detail—in football or in life—he had no context for the funeral and floated through it numb and rudderless. Nobody knew Deuce better than Ademar, and she was as empathetic then as she had been that day in the elevator after Anil's accident, which helped patch some cracks in his foundation. The only bright spot in the trip home came when Ademar told him that West Point had offered her a slot in the next year's class and that she would visit before Christmas break.

Ademar harbored no illusions that she would be kicking footballs at Michie Stadium, and she didn't even play her senior year at Dell City High School. The best part had been going through it with Deuce and T2, and they were gone. But she was a perfect candidate for West Point as it sought to draw students suited to confront an enemy that confounded the old boundaries of tactics, politics, religion, and gender. Ademar was tough enough and athletic enough to pass any physical tests, a fluent Arabic speaker, and a Muslim who maintained a 4.0 GPA and scored almost perfect on her SATs. On top of all that, Ademar and Z won the Texas State High School

Rodeo Association barrel racing championship two years in a row. Almira and Tam had no doubts regarding their daughter's potential but worried deeply about what her life would be like as one of the first Muslim women to attend West Point. Ademar expressed no doubts about the decision, except for those shared with her God when she lay awake in bed.

Ademar and Deuce were in a new world together away from Dell City as they embraced at JFK terminal upon her arrival, and there were no boundaries in what they did that weekend prior to her West Point visit. They saw the Broadway show *Equus* twice, listened to late-night jazz at the Blue Note in Greenwich Village, tried on funky hats at Goorin Bros. in the West Village, walked across the Brooklyn Bridge under a full moon just so they could say they had done it, and made love for hours between the pristine white sheets of the Pierre Hotel, lounging in bed all morning stuffing themselves full of croissants and poached eggs with hollandaise sauce. Deuce struck a serious note on the drive to West Point.

"It's almost like we're—"

Ademar cut him off. "Don't say it."

"Married."

"Deuce, for me it has been written since we were kids. No hurry. Each of us will be tested. Let's hold this feeling, what we feel now, as a place to go when things are really hard."

"I love you."

"And I you."

T2 was not sleeping in pristine sheets in the football dorm at UTEP; as a matter of fact, the only time he changed them was after a trip to Dell City with a bag of laundry for Almira to wash. He didn't have the zest for football or anything else since Sana's death, and he worried constantly about Anil. Try as they might, T2 and Ademar could not penetrate the wall around their brother, who, with his beard and skull cap, did almost nothing but read the Qur'an and surf the web.

Blue had had a litter of puppies the prior year, sired by a yellow lab, and, like his father, T2 took one to UTEP with him. The puppy was an interesting mix, with one blue eye and a serendipitous personality that had him chasing butterflies with as much enthusiasm as he guarded T2. He was all big puppy feet and, at six weeks, narrowly avoided a run-in with a sidewinder curled around the base of a stock tank the dogs favored for an afternoon reprieve from the Texas heat. That's when T2 decided that would be his puppy, and he would name him Suerte, Spanish for lucky. Suerte would run wind sprints at the high school field with T2 and Deuce, the two of them training for the gridiron in the fall, and had a knack for jumping in front of a receiver to bat down a ball. T2 experienced two major setbacks that year, with Sana's death and a knee injury that effectively ended his freshman campaign. But it was impossible for him to sink into any type of depression when Suerte struck the universal position of a dog who wants to play—front legs stretched, butt in the air, and barking. Suerte helped fill the hole in his heart where Deuce, Ademar, and Sana had been for the first nineteen years of his life.

CHAPTER 12

HUDSPETH COUNTY HERALD
BURR UNDER MY SADDLE
A Forum for Anonymous Commentary
from County Residents

A sea of white faces, by some accounts as many as 500,000, flowed from Freedom Plaza down Pennsylvania Avenue to the US Capitol in Washington on September 12, 2009. Unemployed coal miners and steelworkers, rural mothers, cash-strapped farmers, veterans, and gun rights advocates joined the surging mass of radicalized Americans who felt ignored and disenfranchised under the policies of President Obama.

They call themselves the Tea Party, harkening back to the Boston Tea Party protests over unfair British tax policies, and expressions of their pent-up anger in chants and posters should serve as a wake-up call to the "blue state" progressives who were so certain the nation had turned an important corner with the election of its first black president.

Posters with messages like "Impeach the Muslim Marxist" and "We Have an African Lion in the Zoo and a Lying African in the White House" leave little doubt that the election of Obama has kicked a hornets' nest from one end of the nation to the next.

Their firebrands are in many ways the antithesis of their values: Stephen Bannon, the intellectual former Wall Street financier who founded the right-wing news site Breitbart; Richard Spencer, the affluent prep school boy from Dallas who regularly throws up a Nazi salute; and Laura Ingraham, the FOX News commentator who carts her children to Washington's elite private schools in a Porsche 911. They are every inch the same type of cynical self-promoter as Osama bin Laden, only they rely on sophisticated, poll-driven messaging rather than the words of the Qur'an to light a viral fire on the web and in the news.

The cat is out of the bag, and there is no putting it back.

Traditional Republican stalwarts, like Kentucky Senator Mitch McConnell, the Bush family, the evangelicals, and powerful Jewish groups, are caught on the horns of a dilemma as the dark underbelly of the populist Tea Party movement seems to unleash feelings in America from another era. Swastikas have been spray-painted on synagogues and nooses have been tied to trees in universities as a more violent movement has begun to emerge from this new American populism. Pockets of white supremacy, like the neo-Nazis and the Ku Klux Klan, feel emboldened to move into mainstream political discourse as part of the new "alt-right," and they march openly throughout the United States with swastika posters and Confederate flags. Violent white extremists, who have been stockpiling weapons and other survival gear for the day when their worst paranoid delusions materialize, have staged such brazen acts as the attack on the US Holocaust Memorial in Washington by white supremacist James von Brunn, who killed an employee before being wounded and apprehended.

Neighbors seem to be turning on each other in this low-grade Civil War, and there is no better target than Muslims, with their shrouded women and traditional customs that the alt-right brand as misogynistic, sinister, and un-American. The United States is rapidly becoming a radicalized nation, and it is spreading to Europe. Al-Qa'ida and ISIS, with their skilled cyber warriors, find lone-wolf recruits to carry out violent attacks on targets thought to be untouchable: a military recruiting center in Arkansas and a train station in Madrid.

It should not go unnoticed that just a few hundred miles from Dell City, Major Nidal Hassan, an army psychiatrist at Fort Hood near Austin, fatally shot 13 people and wounded 30 more in November.

CHAPTER 13

The day after the shooting at Fort Hood, Anil received a three-word message from Cleo the Leo: "It's your time."

But Cleo the Leo was not the only object of Anil's obsession on the web. In his daily diet of pornography, Anil found a series of videos on Pornhub depicting sex with Juarez prostitutes that he bookmarked and returned to on an almost daily basis. He didn't want to save himself for those seventy-two virgins waiting in heaven for his triumphant jihad, and a heathen Mexican hooker was just the kind of spoil a warrior like him deserved.

Even in Juarez, where anything goes, Anil, with his pointy beard and skullcap, stood out among the drunken college students, street performers, tourists, and cowboys from both sides of the border. Just over the Paseo del Norte Bridge, west of Avenida Juarez, he found the infamous red-light district known as the Mariscal. Anil had done his research but wasn't quite sure what to expect as he walked into the White Lake, where he was greeted by an older Mexican woman in a white nurse's coat. The "pecker checker," who examined every customer's privates for any obvious signs of disease and distributed condoms, motioned for Anil to drop his pants, but the Muslim boy just couldn't do it in such a public setting and made an awkward, stumbling exit. He tried a few other bordellos in the neighborhood—the Palmira Club and the Green Lantern—but management sensed something unsettling in Anil and refused to let him in. With each rejection, Anil's fury rose over what he felt was obviously discrimination and—ironically, given the circumstance he had put himself in—disrespect for Islam.

Anil found himself under a lone streetlamp when a couple of Mexican street kids smoking a joint walked by. Spotting an obvious mark, they approached Anil, certain he would be easy money.

"Toke, *señor*?"

Anil had never smoked anything, in part because he felt it violated Islamic law, but he was in warrior mode now, and nothing seemed out of bounds. Anil was light-headed and disoriented after several puffs, and he nodded when one of the street urchins asked the obvious question.

"*Mujer, puta*?" Anyone who has lived in Texas knows that *puta* means whore, and Anil stuffed a few pesos in their hands.

For Anil, stoned for the first time and absolutely alone, every hallway shadowed something sinister, and every crippled dog was a sign of some kind that he struggled to interpret. A light rain began to fall as they turned into an alley, and the boy pointed to a room above a rickety wooden stairway. The faint sound of the haunting chords from an old song by the Doors floated out of the open door: "People are strange when you're a stranger; faces look ugly when you're alone. Women seem wicked when you're unwanted; streets are uneven when you're down."

There was no pecker checker at the door, only a fat, middle-aged Mexican woman wearing a black garter, red high-waisted panties that could have come from a 1950s Sears catalogue, and breasts that sagged to her waist. Smoking an unfiltered cigarette on a soiled mattress and plucking bits of tobacco from her teeth, she motioned for Anil to put his money next to a water bottle on the table. Anil dropped his wallet as he fumbled with his one hand to pull out the pesos, and the woman picked it up for him. *"Pobrecito,"* she said, which made him want to slap her as she turned up the volume on Jim Morrison. "Women seem wicked when you're unwanted. . . ." Anil stood frozen next to the bed, skull cap still on his head, as she unbuckled his pants and guided his only hand to her breasts. The woman knew every trick, but try as she might, Anil could not perform. She stopped after twenty minutes, lit a cigarette, and laughed in a way that set Anil on fire with anger, with shame. "Women seem wicked when you're unwanted. . . ." As if in a dream, Anil watched himself break the water bottle in half across the side of the table and thrust the jagged glass into her face, slashing down hard, deep into her fleshy neck. She fell backward on the mattress, eyes wide open and hands reaching for Anil, mute from the blood rushing into her throat. Anil didn't wait for her to die, and there would be no justice. Just another senseless murder of a woman in Juarez that nobody would investigate. "When you're strange, no one remembers your name. . . ."

Anil thought it might have all been a dream when he awoke the next morning in the familiar surroundings of his room at home, but the blood on his shirt brought it all rushing back: the music, his impotence, and the broken glass ripping her face, but most of all those brown eyes as she slumped backward on the mattress. He needed to tell someone about it, and Cleo the Leo, the jihadi whisperer, proved an eager audience in an extended exchange on WhatsApp. Anil altered the story slightly to make it sound as if the prostitute had tried to rob him.

"Allahu Akbar! First blood! The bitch deserved it. *Kafir,* unclean, undeserving."

"Allahu Akbar."

"You are a true warrior of the Caliphate."

For the first time, Anil felt the pride of belonging to something, and he was relieved to have been absolved, even though it was for a murder that not a single word in the Qur'an would justify.

"I have a mission for you, an important one for us. DANGEROUS."

"Tell me."

"You have explosives on the farm, yes?"

"Yes."

"You will give them to a man Thursday night in Juarez. Hide them well, brother. Go to the heathen bullfighting arena, and he will text you where to meet. Lose the skull cap for this trip. Allahu Akbar."

"Allahu Akbar."

Dynamite was not used very often on the farm, but there were a few old wooden boxes from Dupont stored in the equipment shed that nobody bothered to inventory anymore. Just to be extra careful, Anil took four sticks from the bottom of the box so it looked as if they were all there if anyone checked. Even though crossing into Juarez from El Paso was usually a nonevent, with guards rarely inspecting anything, Anil hid the four sticks of dynamite carefully in the false bottom he fashioned on a Pelican case. He replaced the skull cap with an old cowboy hat and, feeling a bit like James Bond, trimmed his beard.

Anil had no problems driving the pickup across the Stanton Street Bridge, the "Friendship Bridge," and parked just off Avenida Francisco Villa near Bullring Alberto Balderas. He received a text within a few minutes on his "burner," a disposable mobile phone, instructing him to look for a man with a brown felt cowboy hat seated on a bench in Gran Plaza Juan Gabriel. Just as he walked into the Plaza and spotted the man, another text said to sit on a bench about fifty feet away and leave the case. The drop didn't take more than five minutes, and he was back on Texas soil within an hour, an undercover warrior of the Caliphate home from a covert operation. Anil didn't notice a computer thumb drive on the dashboard until he parked the truck behind the house on the farm.

The dynamite would find its way onto a container ship in the ports of Veracruz or Altamira and across the ocean to Iraq or Afghanistan, where it might be used in a roadside bomb or a suicide vest. But more importantly, the terrorist group had drawn Anil across a threshold from which he would probably not return, at least not alive, a fully radicalized asset in the heart of America.

When Anil plugged the thumb drive into his Mac, he found a detailed itinerary and instructions for a journey to a training camp in Afghanistan. After Ademar left Dell City in August for West Point, Anil disappeared without a trace.

Ten days later, two men who obviously didn't belong in Dell City parked a nondescript black sedan on the cement pad behind the Hudspeth County Sheriff's office, a single-wide trailer next to the water tower and catty-corner from the Two T's Grocery. Deputy Ronin Montoya was smoking a Marlboro on the steps as two men in dark suits stepped out of the car and approached, FBI identification in hand.

"Deputy Montoya, I'm Special Agent Roberts, and this is Special Agent Dunn from the field office in El Paso."

"Yes sir. What can I do for you?"

"We've been monitoring some suspicious internet traffic between Dell City, Europe, and the Middle East. We think someone here named Anil Zarkan may be involved with some terrorist activity. Do you know him?"

"Of course, but wait a damn minute. His family has been here for generations, working for one of the founders of this town."

"We have a search warrant we intend to execute this morning. Please take us to their house."

Ali and his daughter-in-law, Bernia, were on the porch drinking coffee when they saw a cloud of dust at the head of the dirt road from Montoya's white pickup and the FBI agents' sedan, lights flashing but sirens silent. *Shit*, Montoya thought. *Who do they think's inside there—Bonnie and Clyde?*

They stopped in front of the house, and before Montoya could exit his truck, the two agents were squat behind the car doors, Roberts with a Glock 9 mm and Dunn with a Remington 12-gauge pointing through the open windows at Ali and Bernia. Roberts began barking orders on the loudspeaker as Montoya jumped between the agents and the house.

"Stand down, deputy. You two on the porch, on your stomachs, hands behind your head."

Ali stood up in protest, and Dunn tightened his finger across the shotgun trigger.

"Wait, wait!" Montoya shouted at the FBI agents. "Ali, Bernia . . . Just do it."

Bernia helped Ali, north of eighty and arthritic, to the ground and lay down next to him. Roberts and Dunn were on them in seconds, guns in the back of their heads and knees pushed hard into their backs. Dunn dislocated Ali's shoulder when he wrenched the old man's hands behind him to slap on handcuffs, and he touched Bernia during a body search in a way that no other man besides Orhan had ever touched her.

The door to the house swung open, and Jack Laws stepped out, lever-action 30.30 by his side.

Even at ninety, Jack was not to be taken lightly by anyone, least of all two strangers who had just roughed-up his closest friends in the world. Crockett, with a sawed-off, and Tam, who looked as if he could still strap it on for a D1 bowl game, were next, followed by Blue, snarling and clearly ready to take a bullet for the Zarkans.

"Easy, fellas," Jack said. "What's this all about, Ronin."

"My apologies, Mr. Laws, Ali, Bernia. These FBI agents say Anil's in some kind of trouble, mixed up with some terrorists. Show them your IDs, the search warrant."

Jack pushed his Marfa Low Crown back on his head. "Take off those goddamn handcuffs first. Then we'll talk."

That moment could have gone either way, but the FBI agents, well versed in the lessons from the eleven-day Ruby Ridge fiasco with the Weaver family seventeen years earlier in Idaho that had ended in a shootout that killed three people, backed off. Everyone gathered in the living room while the house was searched for several hours and bags of evidence, including Anil's computer, were seized. When they were done, Agent Roberts showed them a photograph of a young man walking through security at Istanbul Ataturk Airport.

"Can you identify him?"

"That's my son Anil," Almira said.

"Well, ma'am, we can't say for sure, but we've seen this before. These terrorist groups recruit here in America. You're Muslim?"

"Yes."

"My guess would be that by now he's in Afghanistan, Iraq, maybe Syria. We'll know more once we get into his computer."

CHAPTER 14

Ademar started her West Point obstacle course test from a three-point stance, like the football player she once was, rather than a running position like everyone else. Deuce hadn't advised her to do it, but he smiled from the edge of Hayes Gym when she did.

Navigating a romantic relationship between a plebe and a sophomore "yearling," particularly a female Muslim plebe and a white yearling, could be as tricky as it gets in the hyper-competitive, intensely Christian environment of West Point. The expanding, foundering war in Iraq and the sickening pace of terrorist attacks in the West by al-Qa'ida and ISIS, which hardened misperceptions about Islam, didn't make it any easier. Ademar didn't have her family, the Laws, and the close-knit Dell City community around her for support. About 20 percent of the 4,400 cadets were women, among them only three Muslims. And deep down, at least that first year, despite all the official command blabber about tolerance and diversity, she knew Deuce was the only person who really had her back.

Ademar didn't flinch when a gob of phlegm splattered in the middle of the first obstacle on the course, a twenty-foot barrier about a foot and a half high under which she had to wriggle on her belly like a crab, and she didn't look up at the balcony to see who had done it. But she and Deuce both knew it was Atticus Jefferson, a black "firstie" fourth-year cadet from New Jersey who played linebacker on the football team and seemed to go out of his way to antagonize Ademar. Shit always flows down.

Ademar flew into the low crawl at a slight angle, enough to avoid Jefferson's spit and to add a precious few seconds of time, which had to be under five and a half minutes for a female cadet to pass and just under three and a half minutes for a male, but made it up and then some through the tires, two-handed vault, and eight-foot horizontal shelf. Ademar was built for it, compact enough at five feet eight inches to leap through the tires and skip over the balance beam, with the strength of a farm girl to lift her 130 pounds easily over the eight-foot wall, across the twenty-foot ladder, and to the top of the sixteen-foot rope. Ademar had almost two minutes to spare when she started the 350-meter run around the oval track above the obstacles, the first lap with a six-pound medicine ball, the second with a baton, and the final one an all-out, hands-free sprint. Respect is earned at West Point, whether you're a man or a woman, and there was plenty enough of it among the hundred or so cadets cheering Ademar as she crossed the finish line at three minutes and nine seconds, a full five seconds faster than Jefferson.

The intense physical side of West Point was not a problem for Ademar, and a lifetime of Zarkan wrestling put her miles ahead of most plebes—man or woman—in the combatives courses. Unlike vanilla self-defense classes at most universities, where women learn to strike and escape, combatives teaches cadets to kill—with knives, feet, elbows, and fingers. With an arsenal of Zarkan headlocks from her youth and a portfolio of soft-tissue strikes from West Point, Ademar would prove to be the equal of any enemy in a hand-to-hand showdown. But if she had to kill, Ademar, who had grown up in the high desert taking down deer and jackrabbits from a hundred yards with the 30.30, preferred to do it at distance with a rifle. She was so good with the standard weapons, 9 mm pistol and M4 carbine, that the coach of the rifle team asked her to join, and within a few months she was among the top five shooters who competed against other schools with the air rifle and the .22.

Although Ademar had received a solid public school education at Dell City High, the amount of work and competition was nothing like West Point. Cadets are required to take eighteen hours of coursework per semester on top of everything else, much of it heavily oriented toward math and sciences, and to survive on about four hours of sleep. Any type of physical romance between cadets is forbidden on West Point grounds, even touching, but Ademar found a platonic intimacy with Deuce in the late-night study sessions where he coached her through academic survival at one of the finest universities in the nation.

It was during "gloom period," those frozen, sunless midwinter months in New York State, when Ademar hit the wall and nearly quit. She was alone in the basement of Davis Barracks fiddling with some of her equipment when Jefferson snuck up from behind and slapped her hard on the ass.

"'Sup, girl?"

Ademar spun around. "What the fuck is that, Jefferson."

"You know you like it, Zarkan. From what I hear, you dune coons like it rough."

Ademar knew she had a split second to defuse the situation or strike the kind of blow that would render a man, a 210-pound Division I linebacker, helpless. She moved closer—slowly, methodically coiling like a rattler about to strike an elusive prey—in a way that Jefferson interpreted as a green light.

"That's what I'm talking about, princess," Jefferson said and began to wrap one arm around her as he leaned in for a kiss, clearly not in a mood to be defused.

Inches apart, within just a few seconds, Ademar raised her knee sharply into Jefferson's groin with enough power to split the uprights on a 40-yard field goal, grabbed his hand, and twisted it until the wrist popped out of joint. She was on autopilot in full combat mode and barely heard him yell. All she saw was Jefferson's face twisted back at her, and Ademar stuck her thumb into his eye with a powerful twisting thrust. He bellowed like a stuck pig, and within seconds several cadets rushed in to pull her off him.

West Point maintains a strict honor code, under which cadets will be expelled if they are found by a regimental panel to have lied, cheated, stolen, or tolerated those who have. The code says plainly, "Quibbling, cheating, evasive statements, or recourse to technicalities will not be tolerated." About 10 percent of cadets brought before a regimental panel are expelled. Within two days, a panel, composed entirely of cadets, had been formed to hash out the true circumstances around the incident in the basement and to render a verdict that could result in expulsion, or even criminal assault charges. It could not have been more sensitive—a fight between a promising female Muslim plebe and a black firstie football star clearly heading up the military ranks— and the most senior levels of the military were watching. The last thing they needed was a call from an investigative reporter at the *New York Times* and a front-page exposé on the politics of gender, race, and religion at West Point. To make matters worse, Deuce had heard in the football locker room that Jefferson, who might lose the eye, had claimed Ademar lured him into the basement to exchange sex for test questions and attacked him when he refused.

Jefferson appeared first before the panel, and Ademar had no idea what he had said when she stood before the nine cadets in the regiment commander's office on the top floor of Davis Barracks. She had discussed it with Deuce for hours, torn between honor and justice, but had not decided until that moment what she would say.

"So, what happened?"

"Sir, respectfully, I have nothing to say, except that I'm sorry . . . sorry it happened."

"Do you understand how serious this is, that you could be asked to leave?"

"Yes, sir."

"And you have nothing to say?"

"Nothing further, sir."

"That will be all, then."

What Ademar didn't know was that Jefferson had done the same, essentially asserting Fifth Amendment rights protecting himself against self-incrimination, and it gave the regimental panel no real option other than to "condition" them both, place them on probation pending any further incidents.

After graduation, Jefferson had a distinguished military career and rose to the rank of brigadier general. Ademar also served with distinction, although her time in the army came to an abrupt end eight years later behind a sniper rifle overlooking a crowded square in Brussels.

CHAPTER 15

Just before dawn on a crisp October day in northern Virginia, two high-velocity bullets shattered the skylight at the National Marine Corps Museum.

Within the span of ten days, bullets from the same rifle were fired at the south side of the Pentagon, a Marine Corps recruiting center, and again at the museum. When the US Park Police apprehended the shooter—Yonathan Melaku, a lance corporal in the Marine Corps Reserve who had immigrated from Ethiopia—several months later at Arlington National Cemetery, they found spent shell casings, bomb-making material, and a notebook with references to the Taliban and to Osama bin Laden in his backpack.

Terrorism was on the rise in the United States, and within a one-year span there were six major incidents linked to al-Qa'ida or ISIS, including a brazen bombing attempt in Times Square. No American community seemed insulated from the growing threat, including Dell City.

Deputy Sheriff Ronin Montoya sat at his desk in the single-wide trailer that served as their Hudspeth County office, sifting through bits of information on the web that might shed more light on terrorist recruiting and operations. He was working closely with the FBI field office in El Paso on the

Zarkan case, and Special Agent Roberts had made available to him some specialized software to assist the probe. There was one program in particular called Crimson Hexagon, developed in partnership with the Pentagon's secret Minerva Research Initiative and a consortium of private concerns that claimed to have expertise on methods to counter violent extremism, that raised questions for Montoya about the fine line between privacy and security. Crimson Hexagon incorporated social science tools, advanced search methodologies, sophisticated satellite heat mapping, and social media posts to identify pockets of potential terrorists, right down to an individual address.

There was no shortage of organizations peddling expensive, unproven tools in the war on terrorism to American and European governments. Even the self-proclaimed international development experts in Washington—whose pipelines of government-funded overseas programs in such areas as community resiliency, education, gender, elections, and livelihoods were drying up—tried mightily to repackage their products as tools to mitigate violent extremism. Leading that pack of government contractors was Global Associates International, where a cadre of former US flag officers, city managers, and data analysts built a focus-group-based model that purported to pluck out sources of unrest that could radicalize citizens, such as erratic garbage collection or underfunded high school sports programs. Montoya attended a meeting at the FBI field office in El Paso with a team of Global's well-dressed, smooth-talking CVE experts and came away from a ninety-minute PowerPoint ordeal thinking they were a "bunch of dime-bag dealers" hawking crack to desperate addicts in some big-city alley.

But Crimson Hexagon seemed different, particularly when it identified a remote line shack a few miles off Highway 1437 just south of Dell City as a potential nexus for terrorism. The software had uncovered compelling results by correlating a suspicious pattern of satellite phone traffic, web searches for precursor chemicals frequently used in homemade bombs, car rentals in Los Angeles by individuals on terrorism watch lists, and gas purchases in Dell City. Montoya regularly checked on an old man homebound by emphysema living alone out that way, and he thought he'd poke around at the line shack after a visit.

All kinds of people ended up in Dell City, like tumble-weeds blown across the high desert into an arroyo, none any more interesting than Dennis Morrison. A former engineer who had designed a robotic cargo loader for the aircraft man-ufacturer that developed the US Air Force's long-range B1B bomber, Morrison, as usual, was watching daytime TV game shows with a sitter. He was always in high spirits, full of jokes or wry observations about world politics, and Montoya learned something new during every visit. Miles away from a modern hospital, Montoya checked that Morrison's oxygen tank was full and that he had shells for the old 12-gauge propped in the corner next to it. Pulling his white pickup out of Morrison's dusty driveway after this visit, Montoya wondered what he would be like as an old man, if anyone would check on him to be sure he hadn't passed. Montoya could be a contempla-tive man, but not too contemplative, and his thoughts turned quickly to the suspect line shack a few miles away.

The US Justice Department had sanctioned the surveillance, but Special Agent Roberts had cautioned Montoya that any type of confrontation or contact with the suspects might dis-rupt an investigation that stretched from Dell City and Los Angeles to Europe and the Middle East. "Just don't spook 'em, Ronin."

Deputy Montoya pulled his truck to the shoulder of the two-lane highway and scanned the shack with his old army M-22 binoculars. The broken-down wooden structure was a good half mile down a dirt road, far enough that the dust kicked up by an approaching truck would be like a Comanche smoke signal for anyone on the lookout. From his time in Iraq as an army infantryman, Montoya had surveilled his share of remote hideouts and knew what to look for, the telltale signs of movement or a glint from glass on the scope of a sniper's rifle. Satisfied nobody was there after twenty minutes, Montoya drove to the shack and parked his truck.

The deputy popped the clip on his 9 mm semiauto pistol to check that it was full, just in case, but left the Marlin 30.30 and the sawed-off 12-gauge on the seat in the cab of the truck. Since he didn't have a search warrant, Montoya was careful about entering the shack or any of the makeshift, tarp-wrapped outlying structures, but so many walls were missing that he could see clearly into all of them. He saw six pressure cookers on a shelf in what could be considered a kitchen and remembered reading in a story on the web that they could be stuffed with ball bearings and fashioned into deadly home-made bombs. He made note of it, as well as some half-burned diagrams of Los Angeles International Airport in a barrel of trash, where he also discovered a computer thumb drive that someone had stomped and discarded.

But they hadn't stomped the flash drive hard enough, and Montoya was able to plug it into his computer for access to most of the files. One in particular, labelled AZ, caught his attention. Although much of it was in Arabic, two English words caught his eye: TNT and DC farm. It didn't take a genius to figure out that AZ could be Anil Zarkan, TNT could be dynamite, and DC could be Dell City. Montoya wanted to run down his hunch before sharing it with the FBI, and he drove out to the Laws's farm. Just after lunch, Jack was napping in a rocking chair on the porch while Crockett and Tam played dominoes.

"Afternoon, Mr. Laws."

"Deputy."

"Found something that might shed some light on what Anil is up to."

All three men stood up on the porch, naps and dominoes instantly forgotten.

"Y'all keep any dynamite out here?"

"Yeah, but it's legal."

"No doubt, Tam. Could I take a look?"

In the big equipment shed about half a mile away, Tam pulled a canvas tarp in the back off two old wooden boxes with the words DUPONT EXPLOSIVES and 17 PERCENT STRENGTH stenciled on the side in faded black ink. Everything seemed to be there when Tam lifted off the lid, but Montoya wanted to see for himself. He didn't find anything amiss in the first box, but he saw that four sticks at the bottom of the second one were gone.

CHAPTER 16

T2 came back stronger and bigger for his sophomore year at UTEP, his knee fully rehabilitated from the injury last season, due in large part to the long runs he and Suerte took that summer across the desert sand near the majestic Guadalupe Mountains.

The Miners got off to a strong start, winning five of their first six games, and T2 contributed on all the special teams. Following a lopsided victory against Rice in early October, in which T2 returned a blocked punt for a touchdown, the coaches began working him in at weak-side linebacker as part of a nickel package on obvious passing situations. After three straight losses to Alabama Birmingham, Tulane, and Marshall, they started T2 against SMU, and the head coach awarded him a game ball for a standout performance in which he made eight tackles and two quarterback sacks. Even though the Miners dropped the final three games of the season, ending with a 6-6 record, they were invited to play Brigham Young in the New Mexico Bowl.

T2 had become something of a celebrity after a feature writer for the El Paso Times profiled the Muslim walk-on linebacker from Dell City who fought his way into the starting lineup for a national bowl game. As part of the UTEP's public relations outreach to the community, sports stars regularly visited local schools, and T2 was headed to El Paso High Wednesday morning before the team left town for their post-season appearance in Albuquerque. He rehearsed some of the talking points the UTEP sports PR staff had prepared for him, two index cards with bullet points on how a six-man player from a Syrian immigrant family in a rural Texas town of four hundred had defied all odds to earn a starting position with a major D1 university squaring off in a high-profile bowl game. Suerte sat on the seat next to him in the pickup for the short drive up East Schuster to El Paso High, his ears perking up every time T2 said *football*, a word the dog recognized as synonymous with a few hours of fun chasing bouncing balls and fast humans.

T2 and Suerte, both of them wearing Miners' football jerseys, stood at the edge of the stage as the principal introduced them to several hundred students gathered for morning assembly. She paused for a moment at two popping sounds outside the auditorium, dismissing them in her mind as backfires from the souped-up engine of some Cholo gang member gunning his low-rider in the parking lot. The principal didn't have a chance to duck when a side door burst open and a teenage boy in a military surplus trench coat fired a fusillade of shotgun blasts at the podium, throwing her violently, headfirst, into a curtain on the back edge of the stage. T2 looked at the principal, the color of her pooling blood the same shade of deep red as the velvet curtain, then back at the shooter, an unlikely seventeen-year-old assassin with greasy blond hair, pimples, and a bandolier of 12-gauge shells across his chest. He was efficient, methodically reloading the gun, pumping shells into the chamber, and firing chunks of double-ought buckshot into his classmates, all of whom he blamed for one imagined indignity or another. *Pop, pop, pop, pop*—three students on the front row seemed to explode in a crimson spray. What only seconds earlier had been the face of an attractive brunette in a cheerleading uniform disappeared, and the arm of the boy next to her came off at the elbow.

Active shooter drills had become commonplace at most American schools since the massacre at Columbine nearly two decades earlier, and they had been refined to three simple words after almost a dozen attacks the past year: *Run, Hide, Fight.* The students in the first few rows, close enough to the shooter to smell the gunpowder from his shotgun, dove behind seats as those farther back scrambled for the exits. The shooter took one step left to a row of cowering students and fired point blank into a boy who held out his hand as if it might somehow stop the buckshot, then into the back of a girl next to him. Run, Hide, Fight.

T2 fought.

Three quick steps, and he was airborne, spread-eagle off the edge of the stage, a moment captured on the school's video surveillance system that appeared the next day on the front page of every newspaper in the country. Two hundred and thirty pounds of college linebacker crashed into the shooter, dislodging the 12-gauge and sending him tumbling ten feet down the aisle. They were both on their feet in a heartbeat, the boy pulling a 9 mm pistol from a shoulder holster under his trench coat as he spun around toward T2, like a character in the online video game World of Warcraft that he played every day. T2's shoulder was into the shooter's ribs hard, but not before he fired three shots from the semiautomatic, one of them shattering a femur and any notion of a football career. T2 recited the passage before death from the Qur'an—"There is no God but Allah, and Muhammad is the messenger of Allah"—as he looked into the eyes of the teenage assassin walking toward him barrel-first. T2 was certain that the smirking, pimply face of the boy was the last thing he would ever see. But he was wrong. Suerte's powerful jaws clamped down on the shooter's wrist and shook his arm until the gun fell away under a row of seats. Within seconds, two school security officers subdued the shooter, and it was over—as were the lives of seven students in a nation moving toward a state of insanity and radicalism so profound that the National Rifle Association would use this tragedy as an opportunity to advocate for arming teachers.

The first images of El Paso High School were being aired on FOX News, with a running headline at the bottom flashing: Muslim Terrorist Attack at El Paso School. A breathless local FOX News reporter with her cameraman ducked under the yellow police tape around the crime scene and jammed a microphone into the face of the deputy mayor helping paramedics wheeling T2 into an ambulance.

"Get this shot!"

"In a FOX exclusive, this is the gunman who a few minutes ago shot up a student assembly here at El Paso High School. Sources have told us that he belongs to a Muslim terrorist group, possibly ISIS."

The deputy mayor interrupted her.

"Let me correct the record for your viewers. This is not the shooter, and he is not a Muslim terrorist. This is Tamerlane Zarkan II, a football player at UTEP who was speaking to the assembly. Mr. Zarkan, a hero, was shot when he tackled the shooter, saving countless lives. And that dog over there, I believe it belongs to Mr. Zarkan, saved his life."

T2 raised his head from the gurney, smiling at Suerte.

"Yes, that's my dog, Suerte, Lucky. And I was lucky to have him with me today."

Suerte, both paws on the gurney, perked up when he heard his name, wagging the tip of his tail and looking to the side in the way that dogs do when they are a little unsure of what's going on.

Fifteen seconds of fame for T2 and Suerte, but they would be heroes in Dell City for a lifetime. Andrew Solomons wrote a long profile about them in the edition of the *Hudspeth County Herald* that came out a few days later, headlined "Our Lucky Day," with a picture of T2 in the hospital and Suerte lying next to him on the bed.

CHAPTER 17

T2 never played another down of football, except for pickup games on the army bases where he spent six years of his life.

The closest he came to the NFL was an invitation from the Dallas Cowboys to flip the coin before their last home game against the Washington Redskins. They made quite a pair in the center of the field, wearing Cowboys throwback jerseys with their names printed on the back—ZARKAN and SUERTE—and almost eighty thousand fans gave them a standing ovation. T2, standing with the four Cowboys' captains, laid his cane next to Suerte when the referee gave him the coin. It was the first time a dog had participated in the ceremony, and Suerte did not miss the opportunity for a little canine mischief, twice snapping the silver dollar out of the air before it hit the turf.

By the time T2's femur had healed, he was in the final semester at UTEP, graduating with a double major in electrical engineering and agriculture. The army recruiter, a big Cowboys fan who had attended the Redskins game two years earlier, sought T2 out as graduation day rolled around and encouraged him to consider enlisting. Bomb disposal experts were in short supply, particularly ones with a background in electrical engineering, and the army was sending far too many soldiers home with arms or legs blown off by roadside bombs in Iraq. He had discussed it with Deuce, who was heading to Ranger School after graduation, and they were hopeful that their combined gravitas as a West Point officer and a high school savior would give them enough leverage to finagle a posting that would bring the two best friends back together. They were reunited at Fort Bliss outside El Paso, after Lieutenant Crockett Laws Jr. earned a Ranger Tab and Staff Sergeant Tamerlane Zarkan II completed a thirty-seven-week course in explosive ordnance disposal at Fort Lee, Virginia. In retrospect, that decision triggered a chain of events that would change the lives of the Laws and the Zarkans forever.

Ademar didn't have much time for loneliness during her final year at West Point without Deuce, between the responsibilities of a deputy brigade commander, the first Muslim woman to reach that rank, school, and training for the NCAA Rifle Championship.

West Point, in twelfth place on the final day of competition at Ohio State, did not have a prayer of winning the shooting competition, but Ademar had a chance for an individual medal after finishing fourth in the ten-meter air rifle event. Collegiate coed teams are composed of five shooters who compete together and individually, much like swimming, from ten meters with an air rifle and from fifty meters with a .22-caliber rifle. The events are tightly structured, with strict rules regarding clothing, equipment, number of shots, punctuality, and time on the firing line.

Ademar had honed her marksmanship in the high desert around Dell City with the 30.30, and she was an ace in these college matches with the .22. All but seven of her sixty shots from all three positions—kneeling, prone, and standing—had touched the bull's-eye, and the only person with a chance of beating her was a woman from the University of Kentucky.

The Kentucky sharpshooter's final shot, which hit dead center on the target, gave her a narrow four-point victory over Ademar. Nevertheless, she returned to West Point a hero after winning the silver medal, the best performance ever by a female cadet. After graduation, it also landed Ademar a position in the elite sniper training program at Fort Benning, where she was just as deadly with the M24.

Ademar and T2 weren't the only members of the Zarkan family rising in the ranks of their chosen professions. ISIS, wreaking havoc in Afghanistan, Iraq, and Syria, relied on sophisticated online propaganda to procure new recruits, bolster morale, and advance its campaign to resurrect a caliphate across land it seized in the Middle East. Cleo the Leo, who was actually a twenty-eight-year-old Egyptian man with a PhD in computer science, recognized a potential cyber-warrior in Anil, and from a remote base in southeast Afghanistan, he became a key part of the ISIS propaganda machine. Anil was as adept at lurking through the backdoors of every popular online game as he was at manipulating multimedia production software, and he was putting the finishing touches on a series of videos unprecedented in their brutality and polished messaging. The first installment in the Clanging of the Swords' franchise, a forty-nine-minute compilation of bombings, beheadings, military assaults, and graphic-heavy propaganda to a slick soundtrack of Qur'anic chanting, was released in August. With the help of content-boosting functionality on Google, Facebook, and Twitter, Anil's video went viral in a few weeks. He had found a chink in the glittering armor of the social media companies, all of which had grown well beyond their abilities to monitor the deluge of daily content and refused to bow under government pressure to assume a monitoring role that struck them as inconsistent with the democratizing principles of the web. Anil had become the rock star of the Caliphate and a bête noire of the West, and he crisscrossed the Middle East like some kind of modern-day Joseph Goebbels to the most senior ISIS leadership.

Anil never imagined that a day could come when he would be asked to pay the highest price of an ISIS warrior.

CHAPTER 18

A day of reckoning had come for the Laws in their risky three-decade play with West Texas water rights. They were all in, and the Texas Supreme Court was about to turn over the final card.

Jack and Marcie—the World War II hero and the corporate agronomist—had bought more than one hundred thousand acres of high desert ninety miles east of El Paso, prospectors in search of hidden water where they could pioneer a farming community in a small town named Dell City. The nation was all can-do exuberance following the victory in World War II, and the Laws had come a long way toward the American dream based on the hard facts of science Marcie had uncovered. The land they purchased sat on top of the hundred-square-mile Bone Springs–Victorio Peak Aquifer, an endless source of pure water fed by snowmelt from the Sacramento Mountains across the Texas border in New Mexico. Marcie was right; as Jack liked to say, "Marcie is always right," and they built a West Texas farming empire on cotton, cantaloupes, potatoes, sorghum, and green chili peppers. They had the unlikeliest of partners in the bloody, bare-knuckled fight, a family of Muslim Syrian immigrants whose founder had come to West Texas in the 1800s as part of President

Franklin Pierce's failed attempt to create a US Army Camel Corps. Together, amid the rattlesnakes, cactus, desperadoes, and grifters of West Texas, they raised three generations of children who would all, in their own way, leave an indelible mark in the world.

Ahead of the curve, as always, Marcie saw an opportunity in a growing nation that would be defined by natural resources and worked out a way to commoditize the liquid gold that had sustained their crops. She found powerful financial partners who shared her view, and together over three decades, they maneuvered politicians, journalists, judges, and municipal officials to their side. The Laws cut their first deal with El Paso in 2002, selling rights to pump water from under their land for $10 million, a fraction of what they expected to make well into the twenty-first century. Marcie and Jack had found a backdoor escape from a way of life that was losing ground daily to the global titans of corporate agriculture. But they hadn't counted on double-dealing lawyers and legions of well-organized smallholder farmers across Texas who feared their water would run dry, leaving them with nothing but a few acres of worthless scrub. The whole house of cards teetered on an old rule that gave farmers like the Laws "the right of capture" over as much water as they could pump, which opponents argued in courts across Texas should be limited to an average of what a working farm actually used over ten years. The Laws had downsized their operation so much over the years that it could be a stretch to claim they operated a working farm, and the amount of water they used the past decade wouldn't be enough for El Paso to brush its teeth.

It all came down to the morning of February 24, 2012, and a ruling on that key question in a related case—Edwards Aquifer Authority v. Burrell Day and Joel McDaniel—by the Texas Supreme Court that would seal the fate of the Laws and their sixty-year odyssey in the high desert of West Texas.

Jack and Marcie, both of them over ninety, looked every inch like Texas farming royalty as they sat next to each other on a leather couch under a pair of longhorns mounted on the wall behind them at the Driskill Hotel, a few blocks from the Supreme Court in Austin. Jack and Marcie weren't formal people, but at Eula's suggestion they had "gussied up" for the occasion—Jack in a dark suit, starched white shirt with a gold Rolex Oyster Perpetual peeking out from under the sleeve, and his best black cowboy boots, the $1,500 hand-made Luccheses Marcie had given him when they'd struck that first water deal with El Paso. And Marcie wore an open, calf-length gray silk coat over a white silk chemise and white linen pants that tapered at her open-toed white heels. A string of white South Sea pearls hung elegantly below her neck, with a pair of matching earrings set in gold, all of which Jack had bought her for their fiftieth anniversary twenty-four years earlier.

Even though it was before noon, they had ordered a stiff drink while they waited for the lawyer to call with the Supreme Court ruling, a double shot of vintage Patron Gran Platinum for Jack and two fingers of Dalmore fifty-year-old single malt for Marcie, neat. Marcie sipped her scotch and placed the crystal tumbler on the polished walnut slab table next to the mobile phone, laying her hand across Jack's.

"Quite a ride, cowboy."

Jack patted Marcie's hand softly and looked at her with those smiling blue Irish eyes that had snatched her heart so many years ago in California. "And then some, Marcelina, and then some."

"Poor Ray."

"We weren't perfect, did our best, and the rest of them are okay . . . Eulalia, Crockett, Deuce."

"I sure miss Sana. She'd have been here . . . and Ali, if he wasn't all crippled up."

"That old boy and I have been through it together. Never told you about what we did to those rapists in Juarez."

"I've known for years, Jack Laws. . . . That's one reckoning all of us will have with our God."

The phone buzzed, and Jack let it buzz again while he threw back his double shot of tequila. He picked it up on the fourth and put the lawyer on speaker so both of them could hear the ruling from Chief Justice Nathan Hecht.

"We decide in this case whether land ownership includes an interest in groundwater in place that cannot be taken for public use without adequate compensation guaranteed by article 1, section 17(a) of the Texas Constitution. We hold that it does."

"Jack, Marcie . . . you win."

CHAPTER 19

HUDSPETH COUNTY HERALD
BURR UNDER MY SADDLE
A Forum for Anonymous Commentary
from County Residents

Our nation is now heading into the holiday season after more than a decade at war.

President Bush's "shock and awe" invasion of Iraq in 2003 began with a bombing campaign by American and British pilots the likes of which the world had never seen, starting with a swarm of precision-guided missile strikes on Saddam Hussein's Presidential Palace.

Operation Iraqi Freedom was launched on a myth spun by Bush, Vice President Dick Cheney, Secretary of State Colin Powell, Secretary of Defense Donald Rumsfeld, National Security Advisor Condoleezza Rice, CIA Director George Tenet, and the neoconservative mob of political appointees that supported them. They had convinced Congress and the American people that Saddam and his weapons of mass destruction were a global threat. But most of the world wasn't buying it, even after Powell pulled out a mock vial of anthrax during a meeting with the UN Security Council in a lame attempt to illustrate the severity of the threat.

The superior firepower and technology of coalition forces— 190,000 Americans, 45,000 Brits, 2,000 Australians and 200 Poles assisted by indigenous Kurdish Peshmerga guerrillas— took down Saddam in two months. And Bush swooped on to the deck of the USS *Abraham Lincoln* off the coast of San Diego in an S-3 Fighter on May 3, 2003, to deliver his mission-accomplished speech.

Ten years later, mired in sectarian violence without a functioning government and at least half a million Iraqis dead, no US official can make a credible case that the Arab nation is better off now than it was under Saddam. ISIS has wasted no time taking advantage of the chaos, graduating to the major leagues of terrorism by seizing and holding almost 70 percent of Iraq's Anbar Province as a beachhead for the creation of their caliphate. The United States is paying a steep price in blood and treasure: 4,000 dead and 30,000 wounded at a cost of more than $1 billion a month, a sizeable chunk outsourced to high-priced contractors.

President Obama, who was elected in 2008 on promises of extracting America from the Iraqi quagmire, fared no better and has deployed more forces in a "surge" to end it, including three of our own from Dell City.

Come next December, let's all pray that they're not still in the Middle East.

CHAPTER 20

That's why Deuce, T2, and their platoon found themselves kicking down doors in the southernmost city of Basra looking for insurgents on Christmas Day 2014.

"Clear," the point man yelled, and T2 peeked into the house in the dangerous, insurgent-controlled slum of al-Hayyaniyah.

Tam held up a single fist and said, "Hold." Five men froze.

Life was worth less than zero in Iraq, and T2 knew first-hand that a family of five in the kitchen was no guarantee that the house had not been wired with explosives. The Muslim family could have been his, particularly the young girl by the sink with the bright eyes that kept darting to a dark corner of the room.

"*Gunbula?*" Tam asked her, using the Arabic word for bomb, then shined a flashlight beam into the corner, where a wire ran from behind a chair and under a carpet. T2 had defused three of these kinds of devices that week, usually a wire connected to the pin on a grenade that would vaporize anyone within twenty feet, and cleared everyone out while he retrieved his ordnance disposal suit from the MRAP parked a half block up the street. T2 had become a master at quickly pulling on the cumbersome suit—almost fifty pounds of overlapping Kevlar, foam, and plastic with a ballistic-grade, visored helmet capable of deflecting shrapnel traveling at two thousand feet per second—but it still took him about ten minutes before another soldier snapped the neck collar in place. Scanning the rooftops for the snipers through the site of his M4 along with the other men in the patrol, he flashed a thumbs-up at Deuce, which his best friend could see clearly since a bomb disposal technician's hands are unprotected for maximum precision when defusing ordnance. "Careful, bro" were the last words T2 heard on his headset as he lumbered back into the house.

Defusing this type of device, a wire attached to the safety pin on a grenade, was much simpler than decoding the innards of a roadside bomb and usually required only a snip. T2 crouched in the corner, cut the wire, and carefully placed the Soviet-era RGD-5 grenade in a blast-proof container.

Tottering out of the house, all hell broke loose as two Iraqi insurgents on the roof across the street opened up with machine-gun fire. A bullet caught T2 dead center on his chest, knocking him ass over teakettle like a blindside block on a kickoff but not penetrating the thick Kevlar armor layered under his bomb suit. Deuce and another soldier dragged T2 to safety behind a wall before he could even catch his breath. Keeping an eye on the building across the street, Deuce, hunkering down for what could be his final firefight, grabbed the radio handset to call for support from an Apache helicopter circling a few miles away. Before he could say a word, one of the insurgent snipers' heads exploded, then the head of the other one next to him. "That's what I'm talking about," a soldier next to him yelled. "Uncle Sam two, terrorists zero. Gotta love our snipers."

This wasn't just any army sniper, which T2 and Deuce discovered a few hours later when they returned to their base. Alone at a table in the mess hall, polishing the Leopold scope on a M24 sniper rifle, sat their most unlikely savior: Lieutenant Ademar Zarkan. Technically under army regs, women were not allowed in combat, and lieutenants were not snipers, but Ademar's commanding officer had bent the rules a bit for a military policewoman, particularly one who had finished second at the National Rifle Championships two years ago.

Nine thousand miles and eight time zones west, another scope was being polished.

Deputy Sheriff Ronin Montoya and FBI Special Agent Roberts were checking their weapons after watching a gruesome ISIS video of a captured Jordanian pilot burned alive in a cage while dozens of hooded, heavily armed militants stood by. The production quality was flawless, complete with slow motion, sophisticated shot blocking, and an ominous soundtrack as the gas-doused pilot danced in the flames until his charred, lifeless body slumped to his knees, then to his back on the floor of the cage. Montoya and Roberts could not have known that Anil was the executive producer.

"No mercy today," Roberts said as they prepared to raid the ISIS bomb shack outside Dell City. Montoya, with a five-year-old daughter and a son on the way, thought he'd left these days in the rearview mirror after Iraq: the pre-mission brief, the surging adrenaline, the body armor, and the final weapons check. He had spotted a black van with California plates that morning at the only gas station in Dell City and tracked it to the shack off Highway 1437. They had gathered a mountain of evidence supporting a warrant and now had the right moment to make an arrest. Their plan was simple, didn't account for any resistance, and called for Roberts to approach the shack while Montoya covered him with the 30.30 from behind the open door of the truck parked about thirty yards away.

It went like clockwork, all three of the suspects walking peacefully out of the shack as if they were certain the whole affair could be settled with a good-natured conversation, until one of them rammed a knife into Roberts's chest and another one ran toward Montoya, firing a pistol and yelling, "Allahu Akbar."

Military muscle memory kicked in for the deputy as the windshield shattered, and he took the ISIS operative down with a .30-caliber hollow-point round that tumbled through his stomach, a one-way ticket to those seventy-two virgins. The one with the knife squatted over Roberts, yanking the FBI man's head back to cut his throat like Montoya had seen in an ISIS video on the web. He paused for a moment, smiling, gloating as if he had negotiating leverage over Montoya. "We can talk?" he said.

Montoya had enough time to cock the lever on the 30.30 and place the scope's crosshairs on his target. "Don't bet your life on it," Montoya said, and shot him through the forehead. The third suspect raised his hands to surrender as Montoya stepped around the door of the truck, dropping the rifle on the seat and unclipping the leather strap over the 9 mm pistol in a holster on his belt. Like two gunfighters in an Old West classic, Montoya and the suspect squared off ten yards apart, neither of them sure what the other had up his sleeve. It wasn't up his sleeve, but stuck in his belt, and Montoya killed the suspect as he went for the gun.

Montoya stood motionless for a moment, surveying the three dead bodies as the smoke from his gun blew in the desert wind. Roberts groaned. "Nice work, deputy, or should I call you fucking Wild Bill Hickok?" The knife had gone deep into Roberts's chest and would have been fatal if Montoya hadn't been there to call in a chopper medivac from El Paso.

Andrew Solomons hadn't covered a story like this since he was a cop-shop stringer in Rhode Island for the *Providence Journal*, and he was heartened that the old adrenaline was still there at almost eighty. The first sentence of the story, the lede, in the *Hudspeth County Herald* the next day said it all: "Like Wyatt Earp at the OK Corral, Hudspeth County Deputy Sheriff Ronin Montoya was the last man standing in a Dell City gunfight yesterday that left three suspected ISIS terrorists dead and an FBI agent critically wounded."

CHAPTER 21

Try as he might, Deuce could not remember how he'd ended up zip-tied to a wooden post at the back of a cave in eastern Afghanistan or how the six-inch gash had opened behind his ear.

The last thing he remembered was telling T2, pulling night duty on the perimeter of Forward Operating Base Fenty in Nangahar Province, that he was going outside the wire to check a fence section that looked as if it needed reinforcement. He was squatting in the dirt inspecting the damaged section; then his memory was a black hole until he woke up in the cave, along with a dozen men—eight Afghans, two Arabs, and two Uzbeks.

T2, Ademar, and Deuce had become a package deal coveted by captains for their units: the ordnance disposal expert, the sharpshooting military policewoman—both of them Muslim Arabic speakers—and the West Point lieutenant with a Ranger Tab. Like a superstitious baseball player who wears the same sleeves under his uniform all season, a squad always took it as a good omen when the three of them showed up for an assignment. They had expected a few years stationed at Fort Bliss, ninety minutes from Dell City, after Iraq. And like a majority of voters, they'd had faith President Obama would keep his pledge to wind down military adventurism in the Middle East and South Asia. Those hopes went largely unfulfilled for eight years, due mainly to misjudgments by the intelligence community on the potency of ISIS, and Americans were now choosing for president between Crooked Hillary and a rich game-show host with a penchant for bigotry. Thousands of soldiers had been redeployed, T2, Ademar, and Deuce for the second time.

Anil had also been deployed, at his request, to launch a new media campaign and to learn the dark art of bomb making. Syria was a meat grinder for ISIS foot soldiers—with drones, cruise missiles, and special forces' strikes sending dozens a month to collect on their seventy-two virgins. That virgin story, particularly for Western recruits who had been with a woman, was wearing thin, and Anil had grown concerned with the social media metrics of his digital franchises. He needed another viral blockbuster like the videotaped incineration of that caged Jordanian pilot to bolster the street cred of the Caliphate. Anil sensed a propaganda opportunity from the union in Afghanistan of ISIS and the Taliban, different strains of Islam, which could open up new regions for recruiting. But that narrative thread lacked punch, decent b-roll at best, and probably wouldn't even merit a share on Facebook for a disgruntled seventeen-year-old Muslim. He was looking for a hard open, something to shake Western resolve and procure misguided youth from their lives of quiet desperation in the suburban Muslim neighborhoods of Paris, London, Brussels, Tashkent, Karachi, and Minneapolis. The answer to his prayers was zip-tied in a cave less than a hundred miles away, and Anil spent the entire journey there polishing storyboards for all the snackable content he could produce from the murder of an American Army officer. Anil had written a script for the captive to recite, and he planned to shoot it at sunset that evening.

Anil could do everything from his Mac: film, edit, mix, compress, and upload to the web. And when he plugged into the best equipment money could buy from the electronic superstores in Hong Kong or New York, Anil felt like God. He found the power to kill intoxicating and became aroused at the thought of destroying families of nonbelievers with the same taunting cruelty he had endured in Dell City.

The captors had moved Deuce to a nearby shepherd's shack and forced him into an orange prison jumpsuit, a replica of the one worn by suspected terrorists detained indefinitely without charge at the US military prison in Guantanamo Bay, Cuba. Anil was not one for the dirty work and orchestrated these productions from a remote location via video feed—a marionettist contorting helpless puppets at the end of a string, a diabolical Wizard of Oz, a deus ex machina in a Greek tragedy descending from the heavens to take his victim's head. Anil had decided he would capture the desecration of this American soldier in two acts—a humiliating plea for mercy in the evening and a slow decapitation the following morning. "Ear to ear, gentlemen," Anil told his crew in a preproduction meeting, "and place the heathen's head on his stomach while blood is spurting from this neck. Always makes for a good close."

Deuce knew what lay in store for him, just not when, and he wasn't going down without a fight. He had received extensive training for this type of hostage situation and could only hope for a momentary lapse of caution from the captors to grab a weapon and attempt to fight his way out of this hopeless fix. Deuce couldn't bear the thought of Ademar, T2, and their families watching the final moments of his life, trussed like an animal while some hooded terrorist hacked his head off. Nor could he bear the thought of never again feeling the warmth of Ademar's body and the gentle cadence of her breathing next to him in bed.

Deuce fought every step of the way, squirming and twisting the best he could with hands and feet zip-tied together, but the two Uzbeks were powerful and clearly trained in martial arts to find the most tender pressure points—armpits, groin, eye sockets. A slow trickle of blood ran from Deuce's left eye as they forced him into a chair in front of a camera and gestured to an assistant holding cue cards behind it, with the usual blather about infidels, invaders, injustice, and Allah. Deuce laughed as if T2 had just told a good one on the porch at the farm. "Fuck you. Not a chance in hell."

Anil, concealed in an adjoining room but able to hear everything, thought of this as foreplay and became more aroused when his victims struggled. But the air was sucked out of his sadistic fantasy the second he flipped on the camera and saw his victim—Deuce, who had saved him from the chili picker; Deuce, whom Ademar loved; Deuce, one of the few people in the world who treated him with compassion. Anil froze, no longer the all-knowing Svengali of jihad, but transformed instantly into the helpless, desperate, lonely Muslim kid in Dell City. Anil felt like puking every time one of the Uzbeks pistol-whipped Deuce in a vain effort to force him into reading the script, and he pissed himself when they put a knife to Deuce's throat. "Enough," Anil yelled into the mike, his voice cracking like a teenage boy in puberty, "forget this part. We'll just kill him in the morning."

Between the darkness in the shack and his swollen, misshapen eyes, Deuce couldn't see much, and the ringing in his ears from all the blows wouldn't stop. He breathed through his nose, through the pain, to clear his head and focus on a plan for escape. His thoughts drifted back to West Point, to Cadet Chapel and the stained-glass window with the inscription from Revelation—Quis ut Deus? Who is like God? And he wondered whether God was sleeping at that moment in the way that his mother, Lola Mae, had once told him in one of the impromptu bedtime stories she made up when he was a little boy. God didn't sleep, he thought, nor did the devil.

Later that night, Deuce had the sensation someone was in the room and thought he might be hallucinating when he heard a familiar voice.

"Deuce, it's me, Anil. Don't say a word. No time to explain. I'm freeing you. After that you're on your own. Your base is two to three days west. Trust no one. Travel at night." Deuce felt his hands and feet come free. Anil gave him a back-pack with his army-issue 9 mm pistol, one Soviet-era RGD-5 hand grenade, a knife, binoculars, a headlamp, a Pashtun robe, water, and some high-protein biscuits. Anil distracted the lone sentinel outside the door, giving Deuce a momentary opening to slip away, and then retreated to his sleeping bag in a far corner of the nearby cave. Anil pranced around in feigned high dudgeon when they discovered that Deuce had escaped, and nobody suspected his complicity.

Every self-respecting Texas farm boy knows the stars, and Deuce located Polaris and headed west. He moved as fast as darkness and safety permitted over the craggy terrain to put some miles between him and his captors before first light. Deuce assumed they were skilled trackers, maybe even had a dog, and walked in the middle of a shallow stream for several hours before holing up in a small cave behind a waterfall. T2 would have called it an OIT, old Indian trick. He stayed awake humming country western songs until he nodded off in the afternoon to the soothing sound of falling water. In a dream, Deuce was at the spring-fed swimming hole in Balmorhea, three hours southeast of Dell City, with Ademar and T2. Nothing unusual, he and Ademar laughing at T2's cannonballs off the diving board. After one stupendous splash, Anil surfaced instead of his brother, floating over the water dripping with blood, and ascended into the sky. What stuck with Deuce as he jerked awake was that both of Anil's hands were missing.

Deuce hadn't seen or heard any sign of an ISIS search party when he emerged from behind the waterfall late in the day, and he felt safe enough to take advantage of the light to move faster over the mountainous trails. With a little luck, he could make it to within striking distance of the base by dawn. Sunrise the next morning found him under a rock overhang about a quarter mile from the base, close enough to reach it at a full sprint in just a few minutes, but he didn't dare try until dusk. Deuce had to assume that some of his captors were hiding nearby watching for his return.

Ademar had not slept since Deuce disappeared from the base, except for a few power naps in the sentry tower where she could see across the wide plain all the way to the surrounding crags. Deuce had come to her in a dream she couldn't really remember, and Ademar was certain he was alive. T2, who hadn't left his sister's side the entire four days, faced east to recite Asr, the Muslim afternoon prayer, and added a Dua for Deuce's protection from danger. "In the name of Allah, who with His name nothing can cause harm in the earth nor in the heavens, and He is the All-Hearing, the All-Knowing." Afterward, they both scanned the plain with binoculars one last time before sunset.

"There," Ademar said, pointing to a flash of orange in an outcrop of rocks. "Deuce."

Deuce had located two open-top Jeeps about four hundred yards to his left, one with the two Uzbeks and the other with two Taliban, and knew he wouldn't have a prayer of outrunning them without covering fire from the base. But any attempt to alert the base could reveal his location. Nothing at West Point or Ranger School had prepared him for this situation, but something Coach T taught him back in Dell City might work.

Ademar and Tam thought their eyes were playing tricks when they saw Deuce running in a wide loop parallel to the base, one hand by his side to conceal something against his leg. Deuce's pursuers took chase the moment they saw him and within a minute were less than a hundred yards away. Ademar gasped. "He'll never make it."

Tam placed a hand on her shoulder. "Wait. Look." Deuce, the gunslinging West Texas quarterback, suddenly stopped, squared his shoulders toward the speeding vehicles, and fired a 40-yard strike into the front seat of the lead jeep with the hand grenade he'd been hiding against his leg. Tam had to smile. "Son of a bitch. He's running a naked boot," he said as the jeep exploded. That bit of football chicanery had bought a little time and evened the odds in Deuce's favor. But it was happening too fast for any organized military action, with the Uzbeks in the jeep thirty yards away from Deuce and closing quick. Tam looked over at Ademar, baseball cap backward on her head, staring through the high-powered Leopold scope on her M24 sniper rifle as Deuce broke into a desperate all-out sprint for the base, Uzbeks hot on his heels and firing inaccurately from the bouncing jeep. Deuce, arms pumping like pistons, focused on the main gate now only a hundred yards away and heard Coach T's words in his ear: "Run like a deer." Ademar's first shot hit the driver in the chest, center mass, and the jeep careened out of control, throwing the second Uzbek to the ground. He was up quick with a pistol in his hand and a clear shot at Deuce. But Ademar was quicker, seamlessly chambering another 7.62 mm shell without taking the crosshairs off her target and firing it into his throat at 2,500 feet per second.

CHAPTER 22

"If he'd run like that in the playoffs," T2 told the entire Zarkan and Laws clans gathered at the Gage Hotel in Marathon, "we might have won the state championship."

The three of them had completed their tour in Afghanistan a few months after Deuce's narrow escape from his ISIS executioners, and they had a few weeks of leave before their next assignment. Jack and Marcie sat at the head of the table in the private dining room at the Gage, surrounded by the relics of another era in Texas: a stuffed grizzly bear, a Comanche headdress, an antique Mexican saddle, and the like. They were still vigorous in their nineties, but at that age, any day could be their last, and they wanted to celebrate the two families at least one more time. And it was a group worth celebrating—six war heroes, two of them West Point graduates; an indie music star; and four generations of Syrian American immigrants without whom the Laws could not have etched a farming empire out of the unforgiving high desert of West Texas. It went without saying that there were chairs that should have been occupied by Sana, Ray, Bitsy, and Anil.

They hadn't heard much about Anil since Deputy Sheriff Montoya's discovery of the missing dynamite and the thumb drive that seemed to implicate him in a global terrorist network. Deuce, T2, and Ademar had left out any mention of Anil in their account of the hostage drama in Afghanistan, except in vague generalities to Tam and Almira, but this seemed like the right time for full disclosure. Deuce was the only person in the room who'd had contact with Anil since he had disappeared, and he rose from his chair in a gesture that everyone thought would be a characteristically self-deprecating toast.

"Anil saved my life. I want you all to know that first. But he's gone bad, real bad."

"You've seen him," Bernia gasped.

"He was leading those terrorists who were gonna cut off my head and film it for all of you to see on the news. He's some kind of big deal in ISIS, in charge of all that online stuff they do—murdering and recruiting kids to fight for them."

"But he's alive?"

"Was last time I saw him. I'd be dead now if he hadn't helped me escape. Sorry to bring this to you at dinner, but you should know, all of it."

The details about her son's secret, treacherous life with ISIS were almost more than Almira could take, and Ademar put an arm around her mother. "It's a kind of sickness, like Ray. None of us are to blame. But we should prepare ourselves. . . . There's no happy ending."

With the quickening of terrorist attacks, this type of tragedy was being played out in almost every corner of the world—from Kabul and Aleppo to New York and London. The number of global terrorism-related incidents since 2012 had quadrupled to more than sixteen thousand, resulting in more than forty thousand dead. Although the majority took place in the Middle East and South Asia, almost two hundred had occurred in Europe and the United States, shattering false notions of Western invulnerability. No community seemed immune to the scourge of terrorism, even seemingly safe places like a popular gay nightclub in Orlando, where an ISIS-radicalized lone-wolf gunman killed fifty people, or a satirical newspaper in an urbane Paris neighborhood, where two Algerian brothers who were both French citizens gunned down twelve employees in the name of an al-Qa'ida-affiliated terrorist organization in Yemen. The numbers would be far higher if political expediency did not preclude statistics on homegrown extremism from being counted as terrorism. At the core of their violent radicalism, there is little difference between an ISIS bomber in London and a white supremacist shooter in Charleston.

The Laws and the Zarkans were not political, except when it came to their experiences with water rights, and neither Jack nor Marcie could remember a meal among the many they all shared that veered too deeply into world affairs. But the tale of Anil's descent into radicalized madness, combined with the growing intensity of terrorist attacks in the United States and Europe, dominated talk around the table. And there were three experts among them—Deuce, Ademar, and T2— who had access to the latest intelligence and could speak with authority on violent radicalism, terrorism, and what the world could possibly do to alter what looked like an inexorable march toward anarchy.

As far as kinetic responses, T2, Ademar, and Deuce could not have been in any deeper. T2 and Deuce were preparing for an assignment to Western Europe, where they would train security forces in NATO-allied nations on countering violent extremists and ordnance disposal. And Ademar had been loaned to a CIA operation that specialized in hunting down terrorist cells. After their six-month stints in Europe, all three of them would have satisfied their service obligations and planned on returning to Dell City as civilians. Military and law enforcement approaches to violent radicalism were only treating the obvious symptoms, Deuce explained, and would do nothing to cure the disease. "Like swatting mosquitoes at a barbecue." The root of the problem lay in dealing with the underlying reasons people become so alienated and so incensed that they would do the unthinkable, like turning themselves into human bombs and blowing up a bus full of children. And the stigmatization of minorities by populist politicians greedy for votes, Ademar added, fanned the fire of hatred into an inferno of radicalized flame.

The Laws and Zarkans went to the patio outside the White Buffalo Bar to hear a popular local blues guitarist Eula knew. Tires screeched outside as they sat down, and a party of drunken hunters from Houston, men and women alike, stumbled out of an armada of camouflaged SUVs. The hunting party, which had spent the day on one of those pricey junkets where they sit in a tower shooting anything that moves and booze it up from dawn to dusk, rolled into the bar pumping their fists, chanting, "Trump! Trump! Trump!" Nobody was more distracted than Jack by the ruckus from the hunters in the latest camo gear from Cabela's, and after half an hour of Trump cheers, bigoted jokes, and loud guffaws, he told them to "pipe down."

"What's the problem, old timer?"

"You."

"Maybe it's the company you're with?"

"Pardon?"

"Wetbacks or ragheads—any of them legal?"

"Americans. Soldiers. Family. You got a fucking problem with it?"

Tam, Crockett, T2, Deuce, and Ademar knew what was coming and walked over to the table where Jack, well north of ninety, looked as if he was ready to throw a punch.

"Easy, Abuelo," Crockett said. "Let's just dial it back, fellas."

"We're packing, hotrod, if you're looking for trouble," one of the hunters said as he peeled his starched and pressed field jacket back from his gut to show a silver-plated Colt Python .357 magnum in a leather holster with a longhorn stamped into it next to a fraternity insignia.

Deuce laughed and, turning to Ademar, said, "Just my luck. Survived ISIS, popped by some drunk frat boy with a fatal case of penis envy."

The table of hunters stood up, and things seemed to be going south fast just as Deputy Sheriff Montoya walked into the bar.

"Whoa, Nellie. Thought I was coming for a beer with my friends, but looks like I'm walking into Dodge City. You got a concealed carry permit for that peashooter?"

"Just in time, deputy," Jack said. "Let's just forget it. We're leaving anyway. Don't like the smell around here. Join us at the Sheepherder's back home?"

Ademar turned to her father as they were walking out. "Remember what I was just saying on radicalization and politics? That's exactly what I'm talking about."

CHAPTER 23

Anil stared through the bars on a window in a room at the maximum-security prison outside Pristina, the capital of Kosovo, while a self-anointed expert on countering violent extremism under contract with the US Agency for International Development probed for details about his childhood and internet habits. Anil had traveled a long road to reach this point, and conning a Washington consultant into believing he had been rehabilitated was the last barrier between him and the sweet taste of jihad.

Anil had sailed across the Adriatic Sea from Libya to the Albanian port of Durres and made his way through porous borders to Kosovo, where he had surrendered to authorities in exchange for a two-year prison term and freedom with a clean slate. This was a well-worn path for extremists intent on terrorizing Western Europe, and hundreds of battle-hardened foreign fighters returning from the front lines of the Caliphate—both men and women—had taken it. Some of them were genuine in their desire to return home to normal lives with their families, but many, like Anil, were moles burrowing into the Western European ISIS network with orders to plan high-profile attacks. ISIS leaders, like the elusive Abu Bakr al-Baghdadi, thought of it as a new phase of their strategy, an expedient bit of spin to mask their defeat in Syria. But their tactic was not without merit, yielding rich returns in blood and taking asymmetrical warfare to a level that tied Western governments in knots over practical issues like citizen privacy and freedom of speech. The Balkans were fertile ground for their perverted brand of Islam, and the seeds had been planted years ago by wealthy Persian Gulf "charities" in mosques and schools throughout Bosnia, Kosovo, and Albania.

The Balkan demographics were perfect, with almost half the population under forty and 60 percent unemployment. Deep resentment lingered, particularly among Bosnian Muslims old enough to have experienced the war and genocide of the 1990s, toward the United States and Western Europe. The popular narrative was that the United States had imposed an unfair territorial settlement on Bosnia as a result of the Dayton Peace Accords, rewarding Serbia for its genocide. Every day, Western intelligence agencies were uncovering signs pointing to evidence of ISIS-inspired, homegrown radicalism: propaganda in bookstores, female circumcision, Salafist-funded orphanages in remote mountainous areas, and bomb plots. Suspicions were fueled by an influx of Gulf Arabs, fundamentalist clothing, gated Muslim communities, private mosques, and scholarship programs throughout the Persian Gulf for Balkan Muslims. The Balkan governments, under intense Western pressure, were struggling to find the right balance between protecting the rights of their citizens and fighting terrorism, a tightrope walk that could further radicalize Muslim communities if not managed in a nuanced way. The opening for ISIS operatives like Anil was big enough to drive a truck through.

Conditions at the prison were not bad, certainly better than a cave in Afghanistan, and Anil was a model prisoner—contrite, helpful, and pious. Even though prison officials claimed not to be eavesdropping on detainees, Anil knew better and went to great lengths in discussions with other prisoners to appear as if he was attempting to debunk the ISIS propaganda he had so masterfully created. But in activities Anil knew were not monitored, like walks in the generous prison yard or informal Ping-Pong matches, he spoke to fellow prisoners in a twisted Qur'anic code that demonized the West and enflamed their radicalization.

Anil planned to plug into an ISIS cell in Brussels after his release, but first he had to recruit an accomplice from the prison, someone so benign and distant from mainstream ISIS ideology that suspicions would not be raised. He had targeted Almedina Shala, a female guard at the prison, in whom he sensed all the characteristics for radicalization. Shala was an observant Muslim who still harbored resentment against the West for her husband's death decades ago in the war with Serbia. Unsophisticated and somewhat simpleminded, she had lived alone for years in a small Pristina flat with her cat, Hashim, named after the president of Kosovo, Hashim Thaci. Most importantly, Shala was a longtime government employee with a valid passport who could travel freely throughout Europe. Within a few months, Anil had Shala on the path to radicalization, certain that justice would not be served for her husband's death unless someone in the West paid the ultimate price. He zeroed in on Shala's loneliness with scalpel-like precision, winning her over with promises of everlasting companionship in paradise as a *shahida*, a female martyr who dies waging jihad. In soulful discussions during walks in the prison yard, Anil had persuaded her to advocate for his early release with prison officials and the consultants from Washington and to marry him when they were reunited in Brussels. The thought of sex with her repulsed Anil and brought back disturbing memories of the prostitute he had murdered in Juarez, but perhaps he could put that off long enough for Shala to strap on a suicide vest and detonate herself in a crowd of Western heathens.

Anil's plan worked like a charm, and he walked out of the prison a free man after serving only six months of his sentence. Almost €20,000 was waiting for Anil in his PayPal account, courtesy of the Caliphate, giving him the resources for transportation to Belgium and a stake to put his plan into play. Border crossings could be tricky, particularly since he might be on terrorism watch lists, but he was counting on making it through with his US passport and a few well-placed bribes.

CHAPTER 24

Deuce and T2 walked out of NATO headquarters in Brussels after briefing their European counterparts on Washington's view of the threat posed by ISIS soldiers returning to the West. Afterward, they had a separate meeting with Belgian police and intelligence services on some fresh information indicating a significantly elevated short-term risk of an attack in Brussels from a recently uncovered ISIS cell.

Brussels was swank duty for them, around every corner another restaurant to sample Belgian specialties—mussels, meatballs, croquettes, and fish stews—that would never find their way onto the menu at Rosita's back in Dell City. They had to double their workouts to balance the food and, in Deuce's case, Belgian ales, but it all felt for them like a victory lap before wrapping up their service and returning to West Texas. They yearned for what T2 referred to as "one last rodeo," a little action before turning in their spurs, and it looked like their wishes might be answered in an operation against that new ISIS cell in Brussels.

European life had not been such a cakewalk for Ademar, who counted three kills over four months, all of them during raids on ISIS hideouts in the aftermath of horrific attacks in major capitals. As part of a covert CIA tactical unit supporting European security agencies, she wasn't based anywhere, moving like a ghost from one city to the next with hardly enough time to sleep or eat. Ademar spent most of her waking hours in military command centers poring over intelligence or on stakeouts in seedy neighborhoods where the best she could hope for was a lump of fried fish and a tangle of greasy fries. The only bright spot was a long weekend in Paris with Deuce, and the memory of languid intimacy between the crisp sheets of the Meridien Hotel overlooking the Bois de Boulogne would have to sustain her until they were reunited in Dell City.

Anil had wasted no time putting his plan in motion. Within days of arriving in Brussels, he connected with a cadre of Moroccans and Turks in the neighborhood of Molenbeek, two square miles of dense apartments jammed with more than one hundred thousand people. Just across the canal from a trendy area of Brussels known for boutiques and cafes, the Muslim borough housed the largest European concentration of ISIS foot soldiers returning from Syria and Iraq. Molenbeek was home to the nine men, most of them Belgian or French citizens of Moroccan descent with automatic weapons and suicide vests, who had executed the meticulously planned 2015 attacks on five locations in Paris that took the lives of 130 people, eighty-nine of them attending a concert by the Eagles of Death Metal at the Bataclan Theater. The narrow streets and cafes of Molenbeek, packed with unemployed Muslim men sipping Turkish coffee and smoking hookah, are monitored openly by Belgian police and covertly by intelligence operatives from scores of nations. Anil had been careful to avoid detection, but not careful enough at Brussels Central Train Station, where a Belgian informant spotted him and reported it to the police. They tracked him to the ISIS hideout near the Pizza Royale off Rue de l'Ecole and launched an around-the-clock surveillance operation.

Deuce and T2 had been temporarily assigned to assist the Belgian police and military dealing with the new threat, along with a special operations unit of the CIA. The Belgian commander was not halfway through his intelligence dump when a junior officer walked into the room, followed by several Americans in civilian clothing, including Lieutenant Ademar Zarkan. There was no space for hugs in that setting, but Deuce couldn't suppress a smile.

"Look what the cat dragged in."

"Lieutenant Laws, Sergeant Zarkan, guess they'll let anyone in this joint."

"You know each other," the commander asked.

"Old friends from Texas."

"And my baby sister."

"Lieutenant Zarkan will be assisting us. We are grateful for her support."

The commander explained the situation—referring to Anil as "a new ISIS operative," since his name was unknown to them—and their possible roles should it expand beyond surveillance. In case of an attempted attack, Deuce would help with command and control in the operations center, T2 would stand by on the scene for ordnance disposal, and Ademar would be the "hammer" stationed on a nearby rooftop with her M24 sniper rifle.

The ISIS cell was in the final stages of planning a bombing near the European Parliament during a visit by hundreds of American high school students as part of a tour under the popular Model UN program. They had spent months quietly gathering the components for two suicide vests, the most important being acetone peroxide, a highly volatile substance used in many common household products. They had experience assembling such bombs—essentially an explosive in the inner layer of a suicide vest packed with nails and ball bearings—and studied pages of detailed instructions available on the web. But they waited for Anil to help them with the triggering device, which detonated the explosive material through a low-voltage current wired to the suicide vest from a device held in the bomber's hand. The ISIS bomb-making A-team had mentored Anil in Afghanistan on how to assemble all the deadliest devices, and he knew the best triggering options for any situation. Anil put the finishing touches on the vests while they waited for the arrival of Almedina Shala from Kosovo, who was prepared to carry out the bombing, and spent any free time eating pizza, watching television, or surfing porn on the web.

Shala arrived two days before the attack, wearing a burqa, the robe-like covering used by some Muslim women that shrouds all but their eyes. As a practical matter, Anil had explained to Shala, she would be unidentifiable to security services or informants. As a matter of petty personal pride, Anil would avoid the shame of marrying an unappealing woman so much older than him in the presence of his cohorts. The marriage was simple and quick—in stark contrast to the elaborate affair at the Gage Hotel for Tam and Almira—with no contract, exchange of gifts, or kisses. His ISIS flatmates barely acknowledged the union as they ate cold pizza in front of the television.

Afterward, Anil and Shala went to the lavatory, the only room in the dingy apartment with a door, to consummate the marriage. Shala had not been with a man since her husband's death almost two decades ago, and she had taken great care to be as appealing as possible to Anil, showering, dabbing perfume in the private regions of her ample body, and wearing a revealing lace teddy under her burqa. She wanted this night to be special, even if it was her last on earth. Anil's only experience with a woman, other than those he watched touch themselves on the pornographic website Camster while he masturbated, had been with the prostitute in Juarez, and that had not gone well. Shala might back out of the bombing if this night did not at least come close to her expectations, so

Anil had purchased Viagra at the local pharmacy and swallowed two pills a few hours earlier. Anil lay on the soiled towel Shala stretched out on the bathroom floor and stared numbly at the bottom of the toilet when she mounted him. Even though it was over in thirty seconds, Shala seemed content, and they were back in the main room eating pizza within five minutes. Anil was disgusted and cringed when Shala tried to cuddle on the couch, but he endured by telling himself it would all be a distant memory in twelve hours, when she was reduced to bits of bone and flesh strewn across a Brussels street.

The National Security Agency had picked up some chatter on mobile phones and the encrypted messaging app Telegram, with vague references indicating a possible attack during the visit of the American high school students to the European Parliament. Not enough evidence for a Belgian court to authorize a raid on the apartment, but plenty to launch the plan to defend against it.

All the pieces were in place before dawn the next morning, each connected through earpieces to a Single Channel Ground and Airborne Radio System. The operation was monitored in real time by Special Operations Command at MacDill Air Force Base in Tampa, Florida, and CIA Headquarters in Langley, Virginia. Deuce helped orchestrate the operation in a command center at NATO headquarters, while T2, undercover in civilian clothes with his tools in a backpack, loitered at a comic book store across from the European Parliament on Rue Wiertz, and Ademar surveyed the site through her powerful Leopold scope on top of a building next door. The twelve buses with the American high school students—wearing coats, ties, and dresses for the occasion—arrived as scheduled at ten o'clock, and Deuce's voice crackled on the radio: "Showtime." Ademar and T2 both felt that that familiar jolt of adrenaline, that stomach tightness a soldier experiences just before combat or a football player feels just before kickoff.

"All clear from here," Ademar responded.

It was the calm before the storm. Anil and Almedina Shala, with a suicide vest concealed under her burqa, had been hiding in an alley behind a grocery store adjacent to the buses. "It's time," Anil said, and Shala lifted her veil in an attempt to kiss him, but he turned away coldly. "Allahu Akbar." God is Great. Shala lowered her veil and walked out of the alley, triggering device in one hand under her robe, while Anil stepped from the shadows to gloat over the impending bloody spectacle from a safe distance. He didn't need any artificial stimulants to arouse him for what lay ahead. Shala looked like a black wraith, robe blowing in the wind, as she seemed to float toward the gaggle of several hundred students. The billowing robe caught Ademar's eye. "I've got something."

Shala stopped in the middle of the students and her hand tightened on the detonating device while she recited the Shahada, the profession of faith, in preparation for death. "There is no God but Allah, and Muhammad is the messenger of Allah." But she looked next to her, at a young Muslim girl from Dearborn High School in Michigan wearing a colorful hijab, and froze, a single drop of sweat running down her back. T2 moved close enough to hear Shala whimpering and sensed an opportunity to stop the madness. "Wait," he said into his mouthpiece, and walked to within a few feet of Shala, careful not to spook the students into chaotic flight.

"Allahu Akbar," he said to Shala. "I can help."

"I am a bomb."

"Show me."

Shala lifted her burqa slowly to reveal the suicide vest, then dropped to her knees in tears. "Help me."

The children closest to them moved away, not sure what was happening but certain they were not safe. The crowd parted, and Ademar had a clear view of T2 with his hands raised and Shala on her knees sobbing in the middle of a widening circle of retreating students. "I have a shot," she said.

T2 whispered in his mouthpiece, "Hold off," and motioned for the students to move away. He told Shala to release the triggering device and remain still, lest any sudden movement detonate the highly unstable acetone peroxide. Slowly, carefully, T2 began loosening the vest until it was open. He was sliding it off Shala's shoulders when something that felt sinister caught his eye.

Anil had been watching across the street as the scene unfolded, unaware that the anonymous rescuer was his older brother. "That bitch," he muttered under his breath, pulled on the second suicide vest in his backpack, and strode across the square toward T2 and Shala, like a spider scurrying over its web to consume a trapped, struggling insect. The two brothers were speechless when their eyes met, frozen in a moment that would change everything, forever.

Ademar did not know it was Anil since his back was to her, but she knew she had to take the shot, even though it might detonate the bomb and kill T2. She heard Deuce in her earpiece, "Take her, Addie."

Ademar looked through her scope, noticing something odd: the suicide bomber with his back to her had only one hand. Her heart sank as T2's voice came over the radio, "Ademar, it's Anil. Shoot." For a split second, she pictured a five-year-old Anil proudly displaying his latest LEGO castle in the living room of their house on the farm, and she had to wipe a tear from her eye before pulling the trigger. Anil's left hand, his only hand, the one holding the detonating device, disappeared.

Anil slumped to his knees within inches of T2 and Shala, no hands and no way to detonate the device. He rose slowly and turned toward the direction of Ademar, no idea it was his sister who had fired, and held out both arms as if he were Jesus on the cross. "Don't," T2 yelled, the last words he would ever speak. Anil threw himself to the ground violently, igniting the acetone peroxide and shredding all three of them into small chunks of flesh with thousands of ball bearings blown from the vest. The children had been spared, but Ademar's brothers were dead.

CHAPTER 25

Islam forbids cremation, but it was the only option for T2 and Anil, given the state of their bodies after the explosion. Ademar had a handful of her brothers' ashes that she planned to spread somewhere, and the Islamic crescent necklace T2 wore that had been handed down from Ali, Orhan, and Tamerlane. She carried all that remained of them, from almost three decades of life, in a small pouch inside her backpack.

Ademar and Deuce left the army immediately after the incident in Brussels, a few months before their official separation date but authorized by their superiors on humanitarian grounds. They spent a few strained days together for the funeral in Dell City; then Ademar disappeared without saying goodbye, except to Eula, who suggested India as a place to heal.

Ademar wandered aimlessly around India for a few months, like a zombie, unable to connect with anything—not the ancient grandeur of the Taj Mahal, the sweeping beaches of Goa, or the solemn funereal rituals at the Manikar Ghats in Varanasi—and she felt only claustrophobia amid the teeming, unruly masses of humanity on the streets. She found no peace alone in her hotel rooms and would wake up in a cold sweat every night, haunted by nightmares about the death of her two brothers. Round and round for hours, night after night, Ademar would follow a single blade on a ceiling fan, spinning her tighter and tighter down a rabbit hole away from sleep and into depression. For the first time in her life, Ademar felt like a *kafir*, one who hides the truth, unclean and undeserving.

Ademar didn't begin to see a path back to whatever normal would be until she walked out of the airport in Srinagar. The vibe in India's only Muslim state soothed her after the madcap chaos that rules over most of the country, although she found a certain grace in the way that Hindus accepted their circumstances, particularly in the sprawling Mumbai slum of Dharavi, where families live separated by thin cardboard walls that regularly fall apart during heavy rains. A friend of Deuce's father, a West Point graduate in Dallas who had ascended the tallest peaks in each of the seven continents following his sixtieth birthday, had written of his affinity for Kashmir in a book about the quest. Ademar was moved by his account of walking along the same mountain paths supposedly traversed by Jesus, Mohammed, and Buddha, and she arranged a visit through a Kashmiri friend of his who owned several houseboats on Dal Lake as well as the local carpet factory.

He went by the name of Haji, an honorific title bestowed on Muslims who make a pilgrimage, a hajj, to the holy city of Mecca. Ademar expected a pious, scholarly Muslim man with a long beard and prepared herself for hours of Qur'anic lectures. But that's not who met her at the Dal Lake station for shikaras, the elegant, canoe-like water taxis that transport travelers to the houseboat communities of Srinagar. The first question from Haji, educated during the 1960s at the best Indian schools and the current patriarch of an esteemed Kashmiri family, was whether Ademar favored dry or wet flies for trout fishing. Laughter came easily to Haji, as he chain-smoked Gold Flake cigarettes, and Ademar found it infectious. Despite his elevated stature, Haji moved easily among the working folk of Kashmir, rebuffing with a friendly wave the vendors approaching in their shikaras to sell rugs, shawls, hashish, and other goods popular among the prosperous Hindus and Western expats who frequented his houseboats.

There is a certain hierarchy among the hundreds of houseboats, about the same size and shape as a double-wide trailer but made of wood and adorned with delicate carved lattice, with the best spot at a point in the deepest, widest part of the lake. Naturally, the flagship of Haji's fleet, the one reserved for Ademar, was first in the lineup. British colonial officers once fled with their families to Kashmir to escape the stifling heat farther south in Punjab or Rajasthan, and Ademar could imagine them fishing, hunting, and lounging on houseboat porches over the water, enjoying a cool breeze while sipping cardamom tea and smoking cigars.

But Kashmir, which had been arbitrarily divided when the British partitioned the subcontinent in 1947, is a dangerous military flashpoint between Hindu-dominated India and Muslim-dominated Pakistan, with regular border skirmishes between the two nuclear-weapons states. And like almost every corner of the world in 2017, radicalization had stretched its sinister tentacles into the Muslim communities of Kashmir. In response to the abuses of Indian forces, young Kashmiris organized themselves into militant groups, like the Jammu Kashmir Liberation Front, that staged mostly nonviolent protests. Within a few years, they had been infiltrated by the global terrorist brands, ISIS and Lashkar-e-Taiba, and graduated from protests to bombs. Ademar awoke with a jolt her fourth night on the houseboat when she heard machine-gun fire in the distance, which, like undertow, pulled her back into the sea of anxiety and tension from Brussels. Out of habit, she reached for a weapon in the darkness where there was none. Haji, smoking hookah under a full moon on the front porch of the houseboat, heard Ademar pacing and invited her to join him.

"Not good for business."

"I can imagine. Brings back memories."

Haji knew Ademar had been an army officer and saw the signs of post-traumatic stress. "Memories?"

"Both of my brothers died a few months back. Terrorists. I was there too. Complicated." Once said, Ademar felt as if the lid had been pried off a secret, and it could all come pouring out.

"We have all night."

It was one of those odd juxtapositions of circumstance in India, where squalor resides amid splendor and mercy coexists beside cruelty, the two of them watching tracer fire arc through Srinagar as they drank sweet tea under the stars. There is a certain impromptu intimacy to the road, and Ademar could let down her guard with Haji, recounting for the first time the tragedy in Brussels and the road that led to it from Dell City to West Point and the Middle East. The sun was just rising over Dal Lake when Ademar finished.

"I want to take you for a walk, Ademar."

"Where?"

"No place in particular, just the mountains for a few weeks. It will be good for both of us. Doctor says I should smoke less and lose a few pounds," he said, patting his stomach, "and you . . ." His voice trailed off.

"You lose; I find?"

"Inshallah."

Accompanied by a guide, Amin, and a pony to carry supplies, the first leg of their journey was anything but peaceful. For three days from the trailhead, they had a few other companions—several hundred thousand Hindus on a pilgrimage to the high-altitude Amarnath cave, where they would crawl the last mile on their stomachs to worship a massive lingam-shaped stalagmite. One of the holiest shrines for Hindus, the Amarnath cave is said to be where Shiva imparted the secret of life to his divine consort. The entire three days were odd, particularly the communal ablutions in the morning surrounded by thousands of squatting pilgrims of all shapes, sizes, and genders, but Ademar had grown accustomed to the idiosyncrasies of India and took it in stride. It was different with the sadhus, the wildly painted Hindu ascetics who shed all worldly possessions to roam penniless through India, many of them wearing only a saffron-colored diaper, seeking spiritual liberation. It was not the bizarre appearance and behavior of the sadhus, and the female sadhavis, that both attracted and repelled Ademar but the motivation behind it that drew her to them. In some ways, Ademar thought, she was doing the same thing.

Several miles before the Amarnath cave, Ademar, Haji, and Amin would head in a different direction from the pilgrims, through a series of high mountain passes near the soaring Nun Kun Massif and on to the Buddhist monastery at Ringdom Gompa. Ademar had wanted to speak with one of the sadhus, but even with Haji's help, she could never seem to elicit more than a blank stare. At a fork in the trail, she saw one of them standing on a flat rock in what yogis refer to as tree pose, one leg bent at a ninety-degree angle against the other and palms pressed together at the breastbone. Ademar was several hundred yards ahead of Haji, not sure which fork in the trail to take, and asked him.

"Excuse me, sir. This way to the pass?"

He smiled, and to Ademar's surprise, responded in perfect British-accented English. "Follow your trail. It knows which way to go."

Enlightenment does not come in a flood or a flash of lightning, despite what is written in the Qur'an, the Torah, the Bible, and the Vedas. Rather it seeps in over time, often after an innocuous comment or moment that keeps tapping on one's shoulder as if for attention. Such was the case with Ademar, as she kept coming back to the sadhu's words, mile after mile, day after day, until she arrived at the Srinagar airport several weeks later to begin her journey back home. Ademar and Haji had grown close during their time together, she helping him through the physical side of the expedition, and he guiding her through the spiritual side. There was no real defining moment when Ademar began to heal, but both she and Haji knew, without having to say it, that closure had begun during their time together in the mountains. They stood together one last time in the terminal, the Haji and the American warrior, with only one final question unanswered.

"Where will you go, Ademar?"

She smiled. "I'll follow my trail. It knows which way to go."

Ademar reached the end of her trail several weeks later, after ten days driving through the American heartland, when she pulled her pickup truck into the parking lot at Rosita's in Dell City. She had been craving one of those smoked brisket sandwiches and had a hunch that Deuce might be there for lunch. Deuce didn't even look up when the door swung open. No reason to, really, since there was no chance in hell that the only person in the world he wanted to see would walk through it. He felt a hand on his shoulder.

"Want some company, cowboy?"

EPILOGUE

Deuce, Ademar and their three-month-old son, Tamerlane Laws, drove out to Rancho Seco a few hours before the reading of Jack's will—Suerte in the bed of the pickup, happy to be along for the ride, any ride. Jack had made it to a hundred, barely, the last of his generation to die. He was buried in a pistachio grove at the back of the farm, next to Marcie, Ray, Bitsy, Ali, Sana, T2, and Anil.

Deuce and Ademar smiled at each other as they came to the embankment at the base of the Guadalupe Mountains, remembering that magical night after their high school prom more than a decade ago. T2 should be with them now, as he should have been every day since Brussels, but all they had left of him was a handful of ashes in a small leather pouch on Ademar's lap. She had Anil's ashes too, certain that T2 would not have wanted their brother to be excluded one final time. Their baby, Tamerlane, had inherited the big hands of most Zarkan men, and it was all Ademar could do to keep him from grabbing at the pouches. They stepped from the truck and stood together for a long time, the majestic mountains behind them and the high desert stretching before them all the way to Dell City. The moment was too pure for words. Ademar opened both pouches, and the ashes of her brothers were swept up in the wind, blown together into the desert, into eternity.

All eleven of them gathered in the lawyer's office for the reading of Jack's will: Eula, India, Crockett, Lola Mae, Deuce, Ademar, Little Tamerlane, Orhan, Bernia, Big Tamerlane, and Almira. At Jack's request, Andrew Solomons was there too. The lawyer explained that he had prepared a legal will, but Jack preferred an informal letter.

If the lawyer is reading this to you, then I'm either in heaven with Marcie or in the other place trying to explain my way out of it. You all know I'm not a big talker, so I'll cut to the chase.

Look around you in the room—white, brown, Christian, Jewish, Muslim, Syrian, American, Texan. This is your family. These are the people you can count on, not those clowns in Washington, Austin, Syria, or anywhere else where they tell you how to think, how to pray, who to kill. Each of you has a part of me in you, through blood, blood spilled, or sweat. We make each other immortal, and it's my honor to live on through you. Be good to each other. Protect one another. Hold each other close.

In addition to the distribution of family assets, each of you has an envelope with a note from me and a check for a million dollars. We did real good in that water deal, and I wanted to share some of it, particularly with the Zarkans. None of this would have happened without them.

You have one too, Andrew, with the stipulation that you use it to keep the *Herald* going and, of course, take care of yourself. I always thought of you as a young whippersnapper, but you aren't that young anymore. You deserve a nest egg for your service to Dell City, for keeping us honest all these years, and for putting up with me. There were times when you were a pain in the ass and I wanted to fire you, but Marcie talked me out of it. She understood the power of truth and of history. Marcie was right. She was always right, including about you being the author of those "anonymous" columns in "Burr under My Saddle."

And then there's my 30.30. I had two of them and gave one to Crockett when he graduated from high school, along with that leather scabbard. I was around long enough to see the marriage of Ademar and Deuce but not the birth of their first child. When the time is right, that rifle is for their firstborn. Tell that child it's from Abuelo, who I was, what I stood for, what we stand for.

That's it—my last rodeo. Adios.

Jack Laws

DISCUSSION QUESTIONS

1. What is the purpose of the book?
2. Do you find common ground with the way the narrative arc depicts changes in society from World War II to the present day, and how have our leaders contributed to these changes? What examples of this change have you experienced?
3. With which character in the book do you most closely identify? Do any characters remind you of family or acquaintances? Which ones do you admire, and which ones do you vilify?
4. Could you envision this book as a movie or streaming series? If so, who would you cast in the major roles?
5. As this book characterizes it, do you see increasing radicalism in our society? To what do you attribute it?
6. How do you feel when you see a sticker or sign that says, Support Our Troops?
7. Is violence ever justified?
8. Have you ever contemplated or carried out a violent act? Have you ever been the victim of violence?
9. What does it mean to you to be a citizen of your nation?
10. Is your nation a better place now than it was 10, 20, 30, 40, 50 years ago?

ACKNOWLEDGMENTS

Seventh Flag would never have come to life without the involvement and support of three iconic West Texas families: Lynch, Schwartz, and Smith.

The story of the Lynch family is inseparable from the story of Dell City, and I am grateful that Jim, Laura, and Mick so generously shared their lore in a way that allowed me to wrap a work of historical fiction around it.

Rancho Seco actually exists. *Seventh Flag* was born and nourished there at the base of the Guadalupe Mountains outside Dell City over more than a decade of pounding nails, adjusting solar panels, tending to "perimeter security" with the mythical 30.30, and sipping Tradicional by the fire outside the Pavilion with the Schwartz and Smith clans. A big *abrazo* and *gracias* to Jonathan, Jody, Jon, Tracy, Laurie Darlin', Nancy, and my chief *cabron*, Bobby.

The granularity of *Seventh Flag* would have been impossible without guidance from those unique people who have carved out a life on the high desert of West Texas: Hudspeth County Deputy Sheriff Nick Hanshaw and Sheriff George Deen; *Hudspeth County Herald* editor-at-large and the voice of Marfa Public Radio, Drew Stuart; Dell City Cougars' football coach Joseph Czubinski; high school principal Verl O'Bryant; and administrator Terri Gentry.

The support and encouragement of the courageous, resilient Muslim communities in West Texas and beyond were crucial in helping me understand the complexities of their lives and how to most accurately present them in the context of *Seventh Flag*. In particular, I want to thank Yousef Sher, former leader of the Islamic Center of El Paso, and Assistant Imam Yehia Ibrahim; my good friend and freshly minted American Mustafa Hasnain, Yahya Ehsan and their talented crew at Creative Frontiers in Lahore, Pakistan; and Shaykh Siddiqi, founder of Hijaz College in the UK, who embodies all that is wise, generous, and good in Islam.

My thanks to the current and former members of the intelligence community and armed forces for pulling the curtain back on their unique society, but particularly to Colonel William Ostlund, former director of military instruction at West Point.

The publishing business is a maze within a maze, and I would have never made it through without my trusted agent, April Eberhardt, and publisher Brooke Warner. And thanks to my team of social, digital, and publicity studs: Lukas Sieber, Alan Rosenblatt, Max Martinez , Lee Papert, and JKS Communications.

My life has been shaped by a long line of strong Texas women who, like the character Marcelina Laws in *Seventh Flag*, have "a way with a petticoat as well as a 30.30," particularly my mother, Patricia; Aunt Ida; and Emma D. Payne from Sulphur Springs. I send my gratitude heavenward to them, as well as to my father, Sidney Balman—B-17 pilot in World War II, POW, and Texas builder.

ABOUT THE AUTHOR

An award-winning national security correspondent and specialist in behavior-change communications, Sid Balman has covered wars in the Persian Gulf, Somalia, Bosnia-Herzegovina, and Kosovo, and has traveled extensively with two American presidents and four secretaries of state on overseas diplomatic missions. With the emergence of the web and the commoditizing of content, Balman moved into the business side of communications. In that role, over two decades, he helped found a news syndicate focused on the interests of women and girls, served as communications chief for the largest consortium of US international development organizations, led two successful progressive campaigning companies, and launched a new division at a large international development firm centered on violent radicalism and related security issues on behalf of governments and other stakeholders. A fourth-generation Texan, as well as a climber, surfer, paddler, and benefactor to Smith College, Balman lives in Washington DC with his wife, three kids, and two dogs.

Author photo © Nhu Nguyen, Nhu Nguyen Photography, nhuphotography.com

ABOUT SPARKPRESS

SparkPress is an independent, hybrid imprint focused on merging the best of the traditional publishing model with new and innovative strategies. We deliver high-quality, entertaining, and engaging content that enhances readers' lives. We are proud to bring to market a list of *New York Times* best-selling, award-winning, and debut authors who represent a wide array of genres, as well as our established, industry-wide reputation for creative, results-driven success in working with authors. SparkPress, a BookSparks imprint, is a division of SparkPoint Studio LLC.

Learn more at GoSparkPress.com

SELECTED TITLES FROM SPARKPRESS

SparkPress is an independent boutique publisher delivering high-quality, entertaining, and engaging content that enhances readers' lives, with a special focus on female-driven work. www.gosparkpress.com

Firewall: A Novel, Eugenia Lovett West. $16.95, 978-1-68463-010-3. When Emma Streat's rich, socialite godmother is threatened with blackmail, Emma becomes immersed in the dark world of cybercrime—and mounting dangers take her to exclusive places in Europe and contacts with the elite in financial and art collecting circles. Through passion and heartbreak, Emma must fight to save herself and bring a vicious criminal to justice.

Peccadillo at the Palace: An Annie Oakley Mystery, Kari Bovée. $16.95, 978-1-943006-90-8. In this second book in the Annie Oakley Mystery series, Annie and Buffalo Bill's Wild West Show are invited to Queen Victoria's Jubilee celebration in England, but when a murder and a suspicious illness lead Annie to suspect an assassination attempt on the queen, she sets out to discover the truth.

Sarah's War, Eugenia Lovett West. $16.95, 978-1-943006-92-2. Sarah, a parson's young daughter and dedicated patriot, is sent to live with a rich Loyalist aunt in Philadelphia, where she is plunged into a world of intrigue and spies, her beauty attracts men, and she learns that love comes in many shapes and sizes.

The Opposite of Never: A Novel, Kathy Mehuron. $16.95, 978-1-943006-50-2. Devastated by the loss of their spouses, Georgia and Kenny think that the best times of their lives are long over until they find each other; meanwhile Kenny's teenage stepdaughter, Zelda, and Georgia's friend's son, Spencer, fall in love at first sight—only to fall prey to and suffer opiate addiction together.

A Dangerous Woman from Nowhere: A Novel, Kris Radish. $16.95, 978-1-943006-26-7. When her husband is kidnapped by ruthless gold miners, frontier woman Briar Logan is forced to accept the help of an emotionally damaged young man and a famous female horse trainer. On her quest to save her husband, she discovers that adventures of the heart are almost as dangerous as tracking down lawless killers.